DON
AND
JOYCE
DISCOVER

A Hive of Busy Bees

Dedicated to my young friends at
HERITAGE CHRISTIAN SCHOOL
Indianapolis, Indiana

Many of you will recall these stories which, as your Headmaster, I shared in our morning chapels. Together we considered the claims of Jesus Christ on our lives, and the great need for character-building principles. You were my inspiration!

Many of you have requested these stories. Now I have reorganized and published them for you, and for others across the country.

DEVERN F. FROMKE

*Don and Joyce
Discover*

A Hive of Busy Bees

Stories by
Effie Williams
     and others
Art Illustrations by
James Seward

Building
Christian Character
in boys and girls
5 to 10 years old

Order from:

SURE FOUNDATION,
2522 Colony Court,
Indianapolis, IN 46280

The books in this series have
been published through the
cooperation of Christian
school leaders and teachers
who seek to provide Christ-
honoring and character-
building books for today's
youth.

1998 Edition
Printed in USA
Copyrighted 1987
    by Sure Foundation

ISBN 0-936595-05-1

Contents

"Why the sad faces, Don and Joyce?"

How It Happened

"THE SUN'S gone under a cloud," called Grandpa cheerily over his shoulder, as he came into the dining-room.

Grandma, following close behind, answered laughingly, "Why, my dear, this is the brightest day we've had for two weeks!"

"But look at Don's face," said Grandpa soberly, "and Joyce's too, for that matter"—glancing from one to the other.

"Children, children," said Grandma kindly, "do tell us what is wrong."

No answer.

"Only," said Daddy at last, "that they are thinking about next summer."

Grandpa threw back his white head, then, and laughed his loud hearty laugh. "You little trouble-borrowers," he cried, "worrying about next summer! Why, only day before yesterday was Christmas; and by the looks of the dolls, and trains, and picture-books lying all over the house—"

"But, Grandpa," said Don in a small voice, trying not to cry, "summer will be here before we know it—you said so this morning yourself; and Daddy says he's going up north on a fishing trip—"

"—And so," added Joyce sorrowfully, "Don and I can't go to the farm and stay with you as we did last year, and the year before last, and every year since we can remember."

Joyce looked anxiously from one face to another. Daddy's eyes were twinkling. Mother looked rather sorry, and so did Grandma. But she knew at once, by the look on Grandpa's face, that *he* understood. He only nodded his white head wisely. "I see," he said. And some way, after that, Joyce felt that it would come out all right.

It did.

On the last morning that Grandpa and Grandma were there, Daddy said at the breakfast table—quite suddenly, as if he had just thought of it—"Mother, suppose we let the children choose for themselves. You and I will go to the lake next summer, and catch the big fish; but if they would be happier on the old farm, why—"

"Oo-oo-ooh!" cried Joyce delightedly. "Don, you and I may go to Grandpa's house next summer, if we like!"

"How do you know?" said Don rather crossly. "Daddy hasn't said that we could."

"Why, he said it just now—didn't you, Daddy?"

"Not exactly; but that is what I was going to say," said Daddy, smiling into Joyce's shining eyes.

After that, it wasn't a bit hard to tell Grandpa and Grandma good-by. "Only until next summer," whispered Joyce when she kissed Grandma for the last time.

Long months followed, but June came at last. One happy day the children came home and threw their books down on the table; and Don raced through the house singing the last song he had learned at school:

School is done! School is done!
Toss up caps and have a run!

"And now," said Mother that night, "we must begin to get ready for our trips. Are you sure, children, that you still want to go to Grandma's?"

"Sure!" whooped Don, dancing about the room; while Joyce answered quietly, "You know, Mother, nothing could ever change my mind."

"Very well," said Mother, "tomorrow we must go shopping, for you will need some new clothes—good, dark-colored clothes to work and play in, so Grandma won't have to be washing all summer."

What fun they had in the days that followed! Mother's sewing machine hummed for many hours every day. And at last she got out the little trunk and began to carefully pack away the neatly folded gingham dresses, the blue

shirts and overalls, a few toys and other things she knew the children would need. A letter had already been written to Grandma, telling her when to meet them at the station. And she had written back, promising to be there at the very minute.

When the great day came, the children were so excited they could hardly eat any breakfast. Mother wisely remembered that, when she packed their lunch-box. The last minute, they ran across the street to tell their playmates good-by. When they came back, Daddy had brought the car to the front of the house and was carrying out the little trunk. Mother was already waiting in the car.

It was getting near train time, so Daddy quickly drove off to the station. He bought the children's tickets, had the trunk checked, and then he gave Joyce some money to put into the new red purse Mother had given her as a parting gift. He slipped a few coins into Don's pocket, too, and the little boy rattled and jingled them with delight. How grown-up he felt!

The children were very brave, until the train whistled and they knew they must say good-by. Joyce could not keep the tears back, as she threw her arms around her mother's neck; but she brushed them away, and smiled. "Joyce, dear," Mother was saying, "I am expecting you to be my good, brave little daughter. Take care of Don. Remember to pray every day—and be sure to write to Mother."

Joyce promised; and then, almost before the children knew what was happening, they were aboard the train, the engine was puffing, the wheels were grinding on the rails, and they were speeding along through the green countryside.

Joyce was trying very hard to be brave, for Don's sake. But a lump *would* keep coming in her throat, when

10

she thought of Mother standing beside the train and waving her handkerchief as it moved away.

Although Joyce was only twelve herself, she really began to feel quite like a mother to ten-year-old Don. She must try to help him forget his loneliness. Soon they were looking out the window; and what interesting sights were whirling past! First there was a big flock of chickens; then some calves in a meadow, running away from the train in a great fright. A flock of sheep with their little lambs frolicked on a green hillside; and a frisky colt kicked up its heels and darted across the pasture as the train went by.

By and by, in her most grown-up way, Joyce looked at the watch on her wrist. It was just noon, so she opened the lunch-box; and dainty sandwiches and fruit soon disappeared. But they saved two big slices of Mother's good cake—to take to Grandma and Grandpa.

After lunch, the train seemed to creep along rather slowly. But at last it stopped at the station where Grandma had promised to meet them. And sure enough, there stood Grandpa with his snowy hair and his big broad smile. Grandma was waiting nearby in the car.

It was late afternoon when they reached the old farmhouse, and Grandma soon had supper ready. After supper, Joyce helped to clear away the dishes; and then the little trunk was unpacked.

Grandma was watching keenly, to see if the children were lonely. "Now," she said briskly, "it is milking time. Run down the lane, children, and let the bars down for the cows to come through the lot; and we will give them a good drink of water."

Away scampered Joyce and Don; and soon the cows were standing at the trough and Grandpa was pumping water for them.

"Let us pump!" cried Joyce.

"Fine!" said Grandpa—"that will be your job every evening—to water the cows."

After that, they watched the foaming milk stream into the shiny pails; and then they all went into the house together. It was almost dark now; two sleepy children said their prayers, and Grandma soon had them tucked snugly in bed.

The Sting
Of The Bees

"COCK-A-DOODLE-DOO!" called Don in a shrill voice, dancing into his sister's room.

Joyce opened her eyes and looked about her. The bright morning sunlight was streaming in through the little pink-and-white curtains. "Wh-where am I?" she asked sleepily, seeing Don standing there.

"Where *are* you?" cried Don merrily. "Why, on the farm, of course! Don't you hear that old rooster telling you to get up? There he is," he added, pulling aside the curtain. "He is stretching himself, and standing on his tiptoes. Grandpa says he's saying, 'Welcome to the farm, Don and Joyce!' Do hurry and get up! We must go out and help Grandpa do the milking."

Half an hour later, Grandma called two hungry children in to breakfast. After that, they were busy and happy all the morning long. Joyce helped Grandma to wash the dishes and tidy the house, and Don followed close at Grandpa's heels as he did his morning's work about the farm. He felt very grown-up indeed when a neighbor came by, and Grandpa told him he had a "new hand."

After dinner, Grandma settled down for her afternoon's nap. Grandpa went to help a neighbor with some work, and so the children were left alone.

They began to run races in a wide grassy space in front of the old farm house. But they made so much noise that soon Joyce said, "I'm afraid we'll wake Grandma, Don. We'd better be quiet."

"Let's go to the orchard," said Don. "We can be as noisy as we like there, and she won't even hear us." So away they scampered, to play in the shade of the old apple trees.

But Grandma's nap was not to last long; for soon she was awakened by a scream from the orchard. Hurrying out, she found Joyce dancing up and down, with her hand pressed tightly over one eye. Don stood watching

her with round, frightened eyes. He could not imagine what had happened, to make his sister act like that.

But Grandma knew. Away back in the orchard, Grandpa had several hives of bees. Joyce had gone too near one of the hives; and a bee had done the rest.

Grandma did not say much. Quietly she took the little girl's hand and led her back to the house. Soon Joyce was lying on the couch, and Grandma was wringing a cloth out of cold water and gently placing it on her eye. Before long the pain was gone; but the eye began to swell, and soon she was not able to see out of it at all.

"It's all my fault that we went to the orchard," said Don, looking sober.

"No, it's mine," said Joyce. "I was afraid we would wake Grandma."

"Well," laughed Grandma, "I guess it was mine, because I forgot to tell you about the bees."

When it was time to get ready for bed that night, Grandma bathed the swollen eye again. "I wish there were no bees, Grandma," said the little girl suddenly.

"Why, you like honey, don't you, dear?" asked Grandma.

"Ye-es, I like honey; but I don't like bees—they sting so!"

"Bees are very interesting and hardworking little creatures," said Grandma; "and if they are let alone, they will not harm anyone."

"I didn't mean to bother them," said Joyce, "but one stung *me*."

"That's so," said Grandma; "but they have certain rules, and you must have broken one of them. A bee's sting is the only thing she can use to protect the hive against intruders—and the bee that stings you always dies. That's the price she has to pay to do her duty."

15

"Oh!" said Joyce, "I'm sorry I went too near. But please, Grandma, tell me some more about bees."

"There are lots of things to learn about them," said Grandma. "They live in queer little houses called hives. They have a queen; and if she is stolen, or dies, they will not go on working without her. Only one queen can live in each house; when a new queen is about to come out of her cell, the old queen gathers her followers and they swarm.

"The queen bee lays the eggs; and when the eggs hatch, the hive is so full of bees that it cannot hold them all. As soon as they find another queen, some of them must move out.

"When the bees are swarming, they always take good care of their queen. Sometimes they settle on a limb of a tree; and while they are there, they keep their queen covered, so no one can find her. They send out scouts to find a new home; and as soon as it is found, they all move there.

"Sometimes Grandpa finds the queen, and puts her in the hive. Then she makes a sort of drumming noise, and the other bees follow her inside."

"Was it the queen bee that stung me?" asked Joyce.

"No, the queen never uses her sting except when in battle with another queen bee; but the other bees take care of her, even if they must die for her sake. There are different kinds of bees in the hive. Drone bees cannot sting; and they will not work—they are lazy fellows. In the fall they are all killed, so that during the long winter months they cannot eat the honey which the workers have gathered.

"Bees are busy all the time. On sunny days they gather honey; and on cloudy days they make little wax cells in which to store the honey."

"That's why they say 'busy as a bee,' " said Joyce. "It

means 'busy all the time.' I didn't know there was so much to learn about bees."

"I have been thinking about another kind of bee," said Grandma.

"Do they sting, like the bees in the orchard?" asked Joyce with a little shiver.

"Their stings are much sharper," answered Grandma, "and the pain lasts much longer. There is a hive full of these bees, and they are always very busy. But it is bedtime now. Wait till tomorrow night, and perhaps I shall tell you about one of them."

Ten minutes later Don fell asleep, wondering what the strange sort of bee was like, and hoping it would never sting him as the cross bee had stung Joyce.

Another
Kind Of Bee

"I HAVE something to show you," said Grandma after breakfast the next morning. "Come with me."

"Oh, a little calf!" exclaimed Don a moment later.

"Isn't he cute?" cried Joyce. "See how wobbly his legs are. What's his name, Grandma?"

"Grandpa says he's not going to bother naming him, when he has two bright grandchildren here on the farm," answered Grandma, smiling.

"Does he mean that *we* can name him?" asked Joyce.

"Yes," replied Grandma, "he means just that."

"Oh, Don," cried Joyce, "what shall we call him?"

"I think Bruno is a nice name," said Don.

"So do I; we'll call him Bruno," agreed Joyce.

"I wonder if he would let me pet him," said Don, gently touching the calf on his small white nose.

The little fellow tossed his head and wobbled over to the other side of his mother. The children laughed merrily; and they were so interested in watching the little creature that Grandma had to leave them and go back to her work.

The hours passed by very quickly and very happily—there were so many new things to do! Of course Joyce had to write a long letter to Mother, telling her about the sting of the bee, the new little calf, and many other interesting things.

Late in the afternoon the children remembered about the cows, and they thought they would pump the trough full of water ahead of time. It was such fun that they kept on pumping until the trough overflowed, and the ground around it was all muddy.

After supper, they let down the bars for the cows to come through. The cows had just finished drinking, when Don slipped in the mud and fell backward right into the trough. He kicked and splashed about, trying to get out; and Joyce got a good drenching when she tried to help him. Grandpa had to come to the rescue, and fish him out; and then they all had a good laugh—even Don. The children could not watch the milking that night, because they had to go to the house and put on dry clothes.

Later in the evening, they reminded Grandma that she had promised to tell them a story. They drew their chairs close to hers, and she began:

"It was to be a story about a bee, wasn't it? Well, this bee has a sharp sting, and it goes very deep."

"I hope it will never sting me, then," said Joyce.

"I hope not," said Grandma. "The boy and girl in my story were stung severely; but it was all their own fault, as you shall see.

"Anna and her brother lived near a pond, and when the cold weather came it was great fun to skate on the ice. Oftentimes they would slide across it on their way to school. One morning, as their mother buttoned their coats, she said, 'Don't go across the ice this morning, children. It has begun to thaw, and it is dangerous.'

" 'No, we won't,' they promised.

"When they reached the pond, Willie said, 'Why, see, Anna, how hard and thick the ice looks. Come on, let's slide across it.'

"Instantly the bee began to buzz about Anna's ears. 'Bz-z-z-z-z! Don't do it!' said the bee. 'It's dangerous. You promised Mother.'

" 'We'd better not, Willie,' said Anna quickly. 'We promised Mother, you know.'

" 'But Mother'll never know,' said Willie.

" 'But you *promised*,' buzzed the bee again.

" 'Mother thought the ice was thawing,' added Willie. 'She won't care, when she knows it isn't. You may do as you like, Anna; but I'm going to slide across right now.'

"When Anna saw her brother starting across the pond, she followed, in spite of the bee. But they had gone only a little way when the ice began to crack, and then to give way under them.

"Anna turned and hurried back to the bank; but

20

Willie had gone too far. She saw him go down in the icy water; and she ran to the road, screaming at the top of her voice.

"A man was passing by at that moment. He picked up a board and ran to the pond as fast as he could. And he reached it just in time to save little Willie.

"Dragging the lad up on to the bank, he called loudly for someone to come and help him. Two or three men came running; and they worked over Willie, until at last he opened his blue eyes and asked faintly, 'Where am I?' Then they took him home to his mother.

"She thanked God for saving the life of her disobedient boy, but the danger was not yet past. For many weeks, Willie was a very sick little boy. When at last they carried him downstairs, he lay on the sofa day after day, pale and quiet—sadly changed from the merry, romping Willie of other days. The springtime came; but it was a long time before he could go into the woods with Anna to hunt for

wild flowers, or sail his toy boats on the pond.

"There was no more school for Willie that year. As Anna trudged off alone day after day, she seemed to hear again and again the buzzing of the bee about her ears— 'Bz--z-z-z! You promised Mother!'

" 'I heard it so plainly,' she would say to herself. 'It must have been my conscience. But I wouldn't listen— and I *almost* lost my brother.' "

The old farmhouse kitchen was very quiet for a moment, after Grandma had finished her story. Nothing was heard but the ticking of the old-fashioned clock.

"I'm so glad it didn't happen—*quite!*" said Joyce at last. "What was the bee's name, Grandma?"

"Bee Obedient," answered Grandma. "It has sometimes stung boys and girls so deeply that the hurt has never healed."

"I can see," said Joyce thoughtfully, "that a sting like that would be far worse than the one I got in the orchard yesterday.

"But," said Grandma cheerily, "this bee will never bother you, if you listen to its first little buzz."

"We will, Grandma, we will!" cried the children as they drifted off to the Land of Dreams.

Honesty
Always Pays

IT SEEMED to Don that he had just fallen asleep when he heard Grandma's cheery voice calling, "Breakfast!" He dressed as quickly as he could; but when he got downstairs, all the others were waiting for him.

After breakfast Joyce dried the dishes for Grandma; and then she helped with the sweeping and dusting. Don helped Grandpa to grease the wagon and oil some harness; and he handed staples to Grandpa, while he mended some broken places in the fence.

The children were kept busy until dinner time; but in the afternoon they were free to do anything they liked. Today, they decided to play house in the orchard; so they got out some of the things that Mother had packed in the little trunk, to fix up their house.

But Don soon grew tired of that sort of play. "Let's play hide-and-seek," he said.

"All right," answered Joyce. "I'll run and hide, while you count to one hundred."

Away she ran, and Don began to count. Just as he said, "Ninety-five," she ran to the chicken-house door. It was standing open, so she stepped inside.

Now there was something in the chicken-house that Joyce did not expect to find. One of Grandpa's pigs was there, rooting around in the loose straw.

The pig was not looking for company; and he was so frightened that he ran toward the door pell-mell. Joyce, standing just inside, was in his way; and as he ran against her, she was lifted off her feet and thrown on to his back. Mr. Piggy dashed wildly out of the chicken-house.

Just outside the door was a large shallow pan full of water, which Grandma kept there for the chickens. Joyce fell off the pig's back into the pan of water; and then she rolled over in the dirt.

Don stopped counting when he heard her screams, and Grandma came hurrying out. Poor Joyce! What a sight she was! And she was so frightened that it took Grandma

quite a while to quiet her sobs. But a bath and a change of clothes made the little girl feel quite like herself again.

That evening when Grandma came up from the milking, she found the children on the porch waiting for another story.

"Very well," said Grandma, "I shall tell you a story tonight about Bee Honest.

"Many years ago there lived three little boys—Joe, Henry, and Charles. They all started to school at the same time. For a long while they kept together in their classes; and they were very good friends.

"But when they were about fourteen, two of the boys —Joe and Henry—began to go out nights; and it was always late when they got home. Charles stayed at home in the evening and studied his lessons for the next day, as he had always done.

"Of course, the difference soon showed up in their school work. Charles always knew his lessons, while Joe and Henry fell far behind.

"When examination time came, the boys begged Charles to help them.

" 'No,' said Charles firmly, 'I will never do anything like that. My mother says that my father wanted me to be honest; and I mean to be.'

" 'Aw,' said Henry, 'your father has been dead a long time; and your mother'll never know.'

" 'I say there's no harm in giving a fellow a lift in his examinations,' grumbled Joe.

" 'It would be cheating,' said Charles quietly; 'or helping you to, and that would be just as bad.' And with that, he turned to his own work, and began to write diligently.

"Of course Charles passed all his examinations with honors; and of course Joe and Henry failed.

"After that, the boys tormented Charles in every way

they could. They called him 'Mother's honest little darling'; and when they saw him coming they yelled, 'Go home and hang on to your mother's apron string.'

"Mother knew, by Charles' sober face, that something had gone wrong. 'What is it, son?' she asked; and Charles told her what had happened. She told him how glad she was that he would not do wrong; and how proud his father would be of such a son.

" 'I shall never be ashamed of you,' she said, 'as long as you are perfectly honest. Sometimes you will find it rather hard; but just wait a few years, and you will see that it pays.'

"Charles had been almost discouraged; but Mother's words made him feel quite strong and brave again. The next time he saw the boys, his honest blue eyes looked straight into their faces, unashamed and unafraid. They dropped their eyes, and hurried away as quickly as they could. They did not bother Charles again; for the principal had heard of their actions, and had punished them severely.

"When school was out, the boys began to think about doing something to earn a little money. Henry was passing the drug store one day when he noticed a sign in the window—'Boy Wanted. Apply in Person.' He went into the store at once, and asked for the job.

"The druggist took him to a little room back of the store. 'Here,' he said, 'is a chest of nails and bolts. You may sort them.'

"The boy worked for a while, and then he said to himself, 'What a queer job this is!' He went back into the store and said to the druggist, 'If that is all you have for me to do, I don't believe I want the job.'

" 'Very well,' said the druggist, 'that is all I have for you to do just now.' He paid Henry for the work he had already done, and the boy went home.

"The druggist went back to the little room, and found bolts and nails scattered all over the floor. He put them back in the chest; and then he hung his sign in the window again.

"The next day Joe passed by and saw the sign; and he too went in and asked for the job. The druggist took him to the little room and showed him the chest of nails, and told him to sort them.

"When the boy had worked only a little while, he went back to the druggist and said, 'Those rusty old nails are no good. Why don't you let me throw them away? I don't like this kind of job, anyway.'

" 'All right,' said the druggist; and he paid Joe for what he had done, and let him go. As he put the nails and bolts back in the chest he said himself, 'I am willing to pay more than this to find a really honest boy.'

"Later Joe and Henry, sauntering down the street

together, saw the same sign in the window—'Boy Wanted. Apply in Person.'

" 'Guess he doesn't want a boy very bad,' said Joe. 'That's no job—sorting those old rusty things. Did you find anything in the chest besides bolts and nails, Henry?'

" 'I'm not telling *everything* I found,' said Henry with a laugh.

"Joe looked up, puzzled and a little alarmed. 'Now I wonder—' he began—but broke off suddenly and started to talk about something else.

"A few days later Charles passed by the drug store and saw the sign in the window. He went in and told the druggist he would like to have the job.

" 'Are Joe and Henry friends of yours?' asked the druggist, looking at him sharply.

" 'Oh, no, sir,' replied Charles quickly. 'We used to be good friends; but something happened between us that

I don't like to tell; and they wouldn't have anything to do with me afterward.'

" 'I'm glad to hear that,' said the druggist. 'I rather think you're the boy I want.'

"For two or three hours Charles worked steadily, now and then whistling a snatch of tune. Then he went to the druggist and said, 'I have finished the job you gave me. What shall I do next?'

"The druggist went to the little room to see how Charles had done his work. The boy had found some boxes lying about; and he had placed the bolts in one, the nails in another, and the screws in a third.

" 'And see what I found!' exclaimed Charles. 'It was lying under those old crooked bolts in the bottom of the chest.' And he handed the druggist a five-dollar gold-piece.

"The druggist took the money and said with a smile, 'Now you may place the bolts and nails and screws back in the chest just as you have them arranged in the boxes.'

"After he had done that, Charles was sent on a few errands; and then he was dismissed for the day.

"A few days later the druggist gave Charles a key and said, 'You may come early in the morning and open the store, and do the sweeping and dusting.'

"At the end of the first week, when Charles received his pay-envelope, he found the five-dollar gold-piece along with the week's wages.

"One morning not long afterward, when Charles was sweeping the floor, he found a few pennies lying near the counter. He picked them up and laid them on the shelf, and told the druggist about them. Another day he found some pennies, a dime, and two nickels. These too he laid up on the shelf, telling the druggist where he had found them.

"About a month later, when he was sweeping one

morning, he found a bright, shiny new dollar. How he did wish he might keep it for himself!

" 'The druggist would never know it,' whispered a tiny voice.

"But just at that instant, Bee Honest began to buzz around his ears. 'Don't forget what Mother told you,' said the bee. 'She said she would never be ashamed of you, as long as you were perfectly honest.'

"Charles turned the shiny dollar over and over in his hand. The bee kept on buzzing—'Never do anything that will make your mother ashamed of you. Be honest! Be honest!'

" 'Yes,' said Charles at last, 'I will.' He laid the dollar up on the shelf; and when the druggist came in, he told him about it.

"The druggist smiled and patted him on the shoulder. 'You are an honest boy,' was all he said. And at the end of the week, Charles found the shiny dollar in his pay-envelope, beside his usual wages.

"A few weeks later, the druggist began to give Charles large sums of money to take to the bank for him. 'I have found that I can trust you my boy,' he would say.

"Charles worked in the store all that summer; and when school opened again, he helped the druggist mornings and evenings. His tired mother did not have to take in so many washings now; for Charles always gave her his money at the end of the week.

"After he had finished school, the druggist gave him a steady job in the store, with good wages.

"'Charles,' said the druggist one day, 'do you remember the day you sorted bolts and nails for me?'

"'Indeed I do,' answered Charles. 'How glad I was to find work that day, so I could help my mother a little! And I shall never forget how surprised I was when I found a five-dollar gold-piece at the bottom of the chest.'

"'I put it there on purpose,' said the druggist. 'I wanted to find out what sort of boy you were.'

"'You did!' exclaimed the astonished boy.

"'Yes; and when you brought it to me, I was pretty sure that I had found an honest boy. But I wanted to be able to trust you with large sums of money, so I tested you still further. I left pennies and nickels and a dime on the floor; and last of all, a dollar. When you picked them all up, and laid them on the shelf, and told me about them —I knew then that I could safely trust you.'

"'I should like to ask you,' said Charles suddenly –'was there a gold-piece lying in the bottom of the chest when Joe and Henry sorted the nails, too?'

"'Yes,' said the druggist, 'each of them found a gold-

piece there; and each of them kept it for himself.'

" 'So you lost ten dollars!' exclaimed Charles.

" 'Yes, lost ten dollars hunting for an honest boy. But it was worth it—for I found one at last!' "

"Is that the end of the story?" asked Joyce, as Grandma paused.

"Not quite," said Grandpa, who had been listening. "Tell them what happened to Henry and Joe."

"Oh, yes; I must not forget to tell you about them," said Grandma. "Soon after Charles started working for the druggist, Henry was caught stealing some things from a department store. He was arrested; but his father paid the fine, so he was allowed to go free.

"But his dishonest habits soon got him into trouble again. He broke into a house while the family was away, and stole some money. He was sent to a reformatory for boys; and he had to stay there a long time. After that, he never could keep a job long; for he was so dishonest that no one could depend on him.

"Joe did not get into so much trouble in his boyhood; but after he became a man he forged a check, and was sent to the penitentiary."

"How much better it would have been," said Joyce thoughtfully, "if Henry and Joe had only listened to the bee in the first place."

"Yes, indeed;" said Grandma, "I have often thought of that; for I am sure the bee talked to them, as well as to Charles."

"Maybe," said little Don softly, "they didn't have a Grandma to tell them how to be good."

"Maybe not," said Grandpa, smiling as he rose to take the little fellow in to bed.

"Didn't they ever change into good men?" asked Joyce.

"I'm afraid not," answered Grandma. "That's the saddest part of the whole story. They felt the sting of the bee as long as they lived."

Because He Left
The Gate Open

EVERY day Joyce and Don went out to meet the mailman; and how glad they were this morning when he brought them a letter from Mother! Mother and Daddy were having a good time at the lake; and there was a picture of Daddy, smiling at them, as he held up a day's catch of fish.

"What a string of fish!" exclaimed Grandpa, when they showed it to him. "And what fine big ones they are!"

"I wish," said Don, "that we could go fishing, Grandpa."

Grandpa whispered something in his ear; and the little fellow began to dance about and clap his hands.

"What is it?" asked Joyce excitedly.

"Only that we're going fishing tomorrow," said Grandpa. "We'll start out bright and early in the morning, take our lunch, and spend the day at the river."

Joyce and Grandma were busy all morning about the house; and in the afternoon they baked cookies, and got the lunch as nearly ready as they could for the trip. Grandpa and Don went out to the garden to dig bait.

They soon had a can full of worms; and then Don
found a larger can, and filled that too. When Grandpa
said they had enough, Don covered the worms with loose
dirt and set the cans out in the shed. Then they got out
the fishing tackle.

Late in the afternoon, Grandma called the children
and asked them to catch a chicken for her, so she could
get it ready for their picnic lunch.

The children asked if they might pick off the feathers.
They had watched Grandma do it so many times, they
thought it would be an easy job. But when they tried it,
they found it was not so easy after all. They turned the
chicken round and round, picking first in one place and
then in another. It took them a long time to get all the
feathers off.

Then Grandma cut up the chicken and put it in a
crock, and took it to the spring house to keep it cool. "I

will fry it in the morning," she said.

How quickly the day had passed by! It was already time to do the evening chores. Grandma was trying to teach the brown and white calf to drink milk from a pail. Grandpa was busy in the barn, so she called the children to come and help her.

The calf was kept in a lot near the orchard. "I want you to drive him to the corner of the fence for me," said Grandma. "Then I will try to coax him to drink the milk."

But the little creature was not so easy to manage. As soon as they had driven him into the corner, he would back away; and off he would go again, across the lot.

After this had happened several times, Don said, "Just wait, Grandma; when we get him into the corner again,

I will hold him there."

So the next time, he grabbed the calf about the neck and jumped on his back. Instantly the calf turned and galloped across the lot. When he reached the farther side, he turned again, and Don rolled off on the soft grass.

Just then, Grandpa came to the rescue. He drove the calf to the corner and held him there, while Grandma coaxed him to drink from the pail.

"We must go to bed early tonight," said Grandpa as they started for the house. "We want to reach the river by the time the sun comes up."

"But you'll tell us a story first, won't you, Grandma?" asked Don.

"Yes," said Grandma, as she sank into her comfortable old rocking chair in the kitchen.

"About another bee?" asked Joyce. "Which one?"

"Bee Truthful," answered Grandma. "Boys and girls who will not listen to him often come to grief—as the boy did that I shall tell you about.

"Little Milton lived on a farm. His father had a number of mules, which he used in plowing his fields. Two of the young mules were very ill-tempered. Milton's father was careful to keep the little pigs and calves out of their way, for fear the mules would paw them to death.

"When Milton was almost nine, a little baby brother came into his home. His name was Marion. Milton loved the baby dearly, and never grew tired of playing with him.

"Their father built a fence around the yard. They were careful to keep the gates of the fence closed, so little Marion could not wander away; especially after the two ill-tempered mules were put out to pasture in the lot just back of the house.

"Late one afternoon, Milton was helping his father in the back lot. Daddy had to go and do something else, so he left the boy to finish the job.

" 'As soon as you have finished,' said Daddy, 'you may go to the house. But be sure to latch the back yard gate.'

"Daddy did not get home until after dark. 'Milton,' he said, while they were eating supper, 'did you latch the gate when you came in this afternoon?'

"Milton knew he had forgotten, but he thought to himself, 'If I tell the truth, I shall have to go out and latch the gate now; and I am afraid of the dark.'

"Aloud, he said, 'Yes, Daddy, I did.'

" 'Are you *sure?*' asked Daddy.

" 'Yes,' said Milton again.

"The little boy suddenly heard a bee buzzing in his ears—'Tell the truth, Milton; tell the truth!' But he said to himself, 'It won't matter if the gate stands open all night; I will latch it the first thing in the morning.' And so he soon forgot all about it.

"The next morning, right after breakfast, Milton's mother sent him on an errand. Marion was still asleep.

" 'Where's Marion?' asked Milton when he came back.

" ' He woke up a little while ago,' said Mother. "After I gave him his breakfast, I let him go out in the yard to play—it's such a bright morning.'

"Instantly Milton thought of the gate; and he went to look for Marion.

"A moment later he heard his father cry out in alarm; and looking toward the pasture where the two young mules were kept, he saw little Marion just inside the fence.

"Daddy ran toward the baby as fast as he could; but he was just too late. One of the mules kicked Marion, and he fell over in a little heap. The mule, seeing Daddy coming, ran toward the other end of the pasture.

"Daddy picked up the limp little body and carried it to the house. The baby lay so still at first they thought

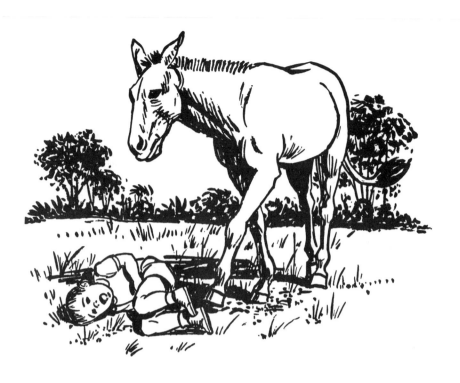

he was dead.

"Milton was terribly frightened, and he cried almost all day; for he knew this dreadful thing had happened because he did not latch the back yard gate—and because he told Daddy a lie about it.

"Poor little Marion was taken to the hospital. His spine had been injured, and it was many, many months before he could sit up. And never again was he able to run about like other children.

"It was a long time before Mother and Daddy found out how the baby came to be in the pasture with the mules. But one day, after little Marion had been brought home, Milton told Daddy the whole sad story.

"'I'm very sorry,' said Daddy kindly, when he had finished. 'I wish you had told me the truth. I wouldn't

have sent you out alone in the dark, son. I would have gone and latched the gate myself.'

"It was almost more than Milton could bear, to have his father talk to him so sadly and yet so kindly. The sting of the bee went deeper and deeper, as he watched his pale-faced little brother day after day. Always after that, he was careful to listen to the buzzing of Little Bee Truthful."

Two very sober children said goodnight to Grandma just as the clock struck half-past eight.

A Wonderful Day
For Fishing

"DON," said Grandma, shaking the little sleeper, "it's time to wake up!"

Don turned over, rubbed his eyes, and with a deep sigh settled back to sleep.

"Here, here!" cried Grandma, shaking him again, "do you want us to leave you at home all alone? We're going fishing today!"

Instantly Don was wide awake. He bounced out of bed and began to dress as quickly as he could. In five minutes, he was in the kitchen; but Joyce was there ahead of him, helping Grandma to pack the lunch basket.

Don was so excited that Grandma could coax him to eat only a few bites of breakfast. He was the first one in the car, ready to start for the river.

The sun was just peeping over the hills, when they drove into a pretty, shady nook on the bank of the river. "This is always a good place to fish," said Grandpa. They stopped under a tree whose great, spreading branches leaned far out over the water; and soon they were untying the fishing poles and baiting their hooks.

"I'll give a nickel to the one who catches the first fish," said Grandpa.

Suddenly Don's cork began to bob up and down in the water. Joyce felt a strong pull on her line, too. Almost at the same instant each of them lifted a fish from the water. Grandpa took a little perch from Don's hook, and a catfish from Joyce's; and with his big, hearty laugh he gave them each a nickel.

The hours passed so quickly that before the children knew it, it was time for lunch. But when Grandma spread

out the chicken and sandwiches and cookies and lemonade in the shade of the big tree, they found that they were as hungry as bears.

After lunch, Grandma lay down in the shade and tried to take a nap, while the others went back to their fishing. But the fish did not bite so well as they had done in the morning.

They had already caught a great many fish, so they decided to go home early. Grandpa had been stringing the fish one by one, as they had caught them; and he had let the line hang down in the water. Now, when he lifted it out, the children were delighted to see how many fish they had caught.

"That is a longer string of fish than Daddy has in the picture!" cried Don.

"We cannot use so many fish ourselves," said Grandpa. "We shall have to share with the neighbors."

When they reached home, Don helped Grandpa to clean the fish. Grandpa skinned the catfish, and Don scraped the scales from the perch. When they had finished, Don had fish scales all over him—even in his hair.

But this trouble was all forgotten at supper time, when Grandma set a large platter of fish on the table. Grandpa said it tasted better than the fried chicken.

In the evening, the children came to Grandma for their usual story. They sat down on the porch, with the soft summer dusk gathering about them.

"I shall tell you a story tonight," began Grandma, "about a bee that every child should listen and obey. Its name is Bee Kind.

"James and Richard lived near each other, and they were playmates. One day they were flying their kites in a vacant lot, when they saw a dirty little puppy. Richard began to stamp his feet and try to scare it; but as he could not chase it away, he threw stones at the poor little thing.

"A stone struck the puppy on his head, and hurt him very badly; for he began to turn round and round, whining and howling pitifully. Richard laughed, as if he thought it a great joke.

" 'Shame on you!' cried James, 'for treating a poor little puppy like that!'

" 'You're a sissy,' said Richard, 'or you wouldn't care.'

" 'You may call me what you please,' said James, 'but I shall never hurt a poor little dog that can't help himself. Maybe he's lost.'

"With that, he lifted the little creature in his arms and carried him home. The puppy's head was bleeding, where Richard had struck him with the stone. James washed the blood away and gave the little dog something to eat, talking to him kindly and petting him all the while.

"When his father came home that evening, he told James that the puppy showed marks of being a very good dog; and that if the owner never came, he might keep him for his own.

"James was delighted. He named the dog Rex, and at once began to teach him to do all sorts of tricks. Rex learned to walk on his hind feet, sit up straight and beg for something to eat, play 'dead dog,' roll over and over, chase his tail, and run through a hoop.

"In a few months, Rex had grown to be quite a large dog. By this time, James had taught him to swim; and when the boy would throw a stick into the water and say, 'Go get it, Rex,' the dog would bring it back in his mouth.

"All the boys in the neighborhood liked Rex; and he liked them all — except Richard. Whenever he came around, the dog would growl and show his teeth.

"Two years later, one warm Saturday afternoon in

44

April, James called Rex and started for the pond. Often-times fishing parties visited this pond, so a number of small boats were tied among the willows fringing the shore. On this particular afternoon, Richard and his little brother Harry had also gone to the pond; and Richard untied one of the boats to take a ride. Of course he had no right to use a boat that did not belong to him; but he thought that no one would ever know.

"Just as James came around a clump of willows, he saw the little boat tip over; and Richard and Harry fell in, at the deepest place in the pond. James knew they could not swim; so he began to call for help as loudly as he could. Rex ran back and forth whining, looking first at James, then at the boys in the water. Suddenly a happy thought struck James. Pointing to the two boys, he said, 'Go get them, Rex!' Immediately the dog jumped into the water and began to swim toward the boys. He soon had Harry's collar between his teeth, and was swimming back to shore.

"James helped Harry to his feet; and then, pointing to Richard, he said, 'Go get the other one!'

"Richard had gone down the second time when Rex reached him; but as he came up to the surface of the water, the dog caught him and began to swim back. It was a hard task, as Richard was heavier than Harry; but at last Rex brought him safely to shore.

"All this time James had been calling for help; and now several men came running toward the pond. They began working with Richard, and after some time he came back to consciousness.

" 'Who got me out of the water?' he asked, as soon as he could speak.

" 'Rex,' answered James.

"Tears rolled down Richard's face as he said brokenly, 'Just think! I almost killed him when he was a little puppy! I know one thing—I'll never do such a thing again.'

"Everybody petted and praised Rex for what he had done. Richard's father bought a beautiful collar for him. But although the dog had saved Richard's life, he never would have anything to do with him afterward. He could not forget how cruelly the boy had treated him in his puppyhood."

"Daddy promised to get a puppy for me soon," said Don. "I shall name him Rex, after the good dog in the story."

"And I'm quite sure," said Grandma, "that you'll always be as kind to him as James was to Rex. But I know a little man that will be asleep in about five minutes. Hustle him off to bed, Grandpa, or you'll have to carry him upstairs."

Don said a sleepy good-night; and sure enough, five minutes later he was fast asleep.

Bee Polite

Who Threw
Those Stones?

WHEN the children came down to the kitchen in the morning, they found that Grandpa had eaten his breakfast, and had gone out to build a pig-pen behind the barn. Don hurried out to help him; and Joyce went to the spring house to do the churning for Grandma.

The little girl plunged the dasher into the thick cream, lifted it, and plunged it again, until her arms ached. At last the dasher began to look clean, and tiny particles of golden butter clung to it and she knew that the butter had "come." Then she took the butter paddle and the bowl and cooled them in the spring, just as she had seen Grandma do. She lifted the butter from the churn with the paddle and began to work it to get the milk out. She had watched Grandma do this many times, and it had looked very easy; but she found it quite another thing, when it came to doing it herself.

After she had worked for some time, she had a solid roll of butter. She salted it, and worked it some more;

and then she called Grandma to come and see it.

"I could not have made better butter myself!" said Grandma. So Joyce had something new to write about, in her next letter to Mother.

After dinner the children went to the orchard to play. They found an ant hill; and it was very interesting to watch the ants as they worked.

One ant was carrying a bread crumb several times larger than herself, and the children were watching eagerly. The old turkey gobbler came strutting toward them; but they did not notice. Joyce was bending over, watching the industrious little ant, when suddenly the gobbler perched upon her back and began to beat her with his wings.

"Grandma!" screamed Joyce.

It was a comical sight that Grandma saw when she came to the door. There was Joyce, running toward the

house, with the gobbler after her, and Don coming behind.

The gobbler was right at Joyce's heels, when suddenly the little girl dodged behind a tree and began to go round and round it, keeping the tree between her and the gobbler. At last Don found a stick and chased him away.

When Grandma had comforted Joyce, she explained that it was the little girl's red dress that the gobbler didn't like. Joyce declared that she would never wear the dress again while she was on the farm. She never did; and so the gobbler did not bother her any more.

At bedtime, the children were ready for their usual story. They clambered up on to the arms of the old rocker on the porch, while Grandpa sat down on the step.

"What do we hear about tonight?" asked Grandpa. "I believe I like to hear the stories as well as Don does."

"All boys are just alike—big and little," said Grandma with a smile. "My story this time is about Bee Polite."

"Oh," said Don, "I know a little verse about politeness. I learned it at school:

" 'Politeness is to do and say
The kindest thing in the kindest way.' "

"Then politeness means kindness, doesn't it, Grandma?" asked Joyce.

"Yes—and more than that," replied Grandma. "A polite person is never rude. The story is about two children who were stung by Bee Polite just once—but they never forgot it.

"Daisy and Dan were twins. When they were babies, their mother took them from their home in the East to live in a far Western state. They could not remember their grandmother, who still lived back in the old home town. All they knew about her was what their mother had told them; and she often wrote long letters, and sent them lovely presents.

"One day they received a letter from Grandma, saying that she was coming to spend a few weeks with them. They could hardly wait for the Thursday to come when she was to arrive at the station.

"The train was due at six o'clock in the evening, and Mother promised the twins that they might go to meet Grandma. After school she sent them to the store to buy some things for supper, and she gave them ten cents to buy candy.

"Now there were some children living in the neighborhood who were very rude. For this reason the twins were never allowed to play with them. But today, on their way to the store, they met these children, and all went on together.

"They crossed a vacant lot, where there was a pile of crushed rock. Near the rock pile, they met an elderly woman carrying a small satchel. She spoke kindly to them; but one of the boys answered her very rudely, and then stuck out his tongue at her. The lady turned to him and said, 'My boy, you need someone to teach you how to be a gentleman.'

" 'Oh, do I?' said the boy roughly. And picking up a stone from the rock pile, he threw it at her. Another lad did the same, and still another.

"Now the twins had been taught to be polite—especially to old people. Just now little Bee Polite began to buzz about them. But when children are in bad company, it is always hard for them to hear the small voice of conscience. For a moment they stood and watched the boys throw rocks at the old lady; and then they began to throw them too.

"No matter how hard she tried, Daisy could not throw a stone straight. But Dan had a better aim, and he threw

a rock which struck the old lady's hand.

"When the twins reached the store, there were several customers ahead of them; so they had to wait their turn. It was nearing supper time when they came out of the store with their bundles. The rude boys had waited outside for them all that time; and the twins gave them some of their candy.

"When Daisy and Dan reached home, they were much surprised to find a visitor there. It was the old lady whom they had treated so unkindly. Mother was crying, as she bathed the hand that had been hurt by Dan's rock.

" 'Children,' she said, 'this is your dear grandmother who has come to see you. She came on an earlier train than she expected; and she inquired the way, and walked out from the station alone. Some rude children treated her very unkindly on the way. You will have to be very good to her, to make up for it.'

" 'Well, well,' said Grandma kindly, 'is this Daisy and Dan? I should never have taken them to be my grandchildren.'

"The twins expected her to add, 'So *you* are the naughty children who threw stones at me.' But she did not say it; and Daisy and Dan hurried out of the room as quickly as they could.

"So the good times the children had expected to have with their grandma were spoiled in the very beginning. After that, whenever they went into the room where she was, they felt very uncomfortable.

" 'I don't understand why the twins act so strangely,' said Mother one day, as she and Grandma sat mending together. 'I am really ashamed of them. They had planned to do so many things to make you happy during your visit. But they seem to keep away from you all they can.'

"Daisy, who was passing outside just under the window, heard every word distinctly. Her heart pounded like a hammer; and she held her breath, to hear what Grandma would say.

"Grandma went on mending, without saying a word. 'Dear Grandma! She won't tell on us for throwing stones at her,' said Daisy to herself. 'Then I'll tell, that's what I'll do!' she added with a sob.

"An instant later, Mother was surprised to see the little girl dash into the room with tears running down her cheeks. She threw herself down by the chair and laid her head in her mother's lap. She was crying so hard that for a moment she could not speak.

" 'There, there, little girl,' said Mother, 'what has happened? Tell Mother all about it.'

"Then Daisy told the whole story. When she had finished, she threw her arms around Grandma.

" 'I'm so sorry, dear Grandma!' she cried.

"Just then Grandma looked up and saw Dan standing there. He had come in so softly that no one had noticed.

"Grandma held out her hands to him; and he burst into tears. 'It was my fault, lots more than Daisy's,' he sobbed. 'I threw a stone before she did; and besides, it was my stone that hit your hand.'

"Grandma talked to the twins for a long time, then, in her own quiet way. She told them that children who were in bad company were almost sure to do wrong themselves; and that polite boys and girls usually grew up to be the best men and women.

" 'I know that such a thing will never happen again,' she said, kissing them both; 'so now it is all forgiven and

forgotten.'

"But the twins could not forget. Two or three weeks later, Grandma went home. She still wrote letters and sent presents, just as if nothing had ever happened. But for many years—long after Daisy and Dan had grown up—every time they thought of their dear grandmother, they felt the sting of their rudeness and cruelty to her."

Joyce winked the tears out of her eyes, as she threw her arms around her grandma's neck. "I could never treat you like that, dear Grandma!" she cried.

"Neither could I," said Don soberly, kissing her goodnight.

Bee Gentle

Why Jake Couldn't Catch The Horse

IN THE morning, another letter came from Mother. "Daddy and I are getting lonesome for you," she wrote.

"We're having a better time than Mother and Daddy are," laughed Don. "If they had come with us to Grandpa's, they wouldn't have been so lonesome, would they, Joyce?"

"I should say not!" answered Joyce. "The days go by too fast for that; and besides, something is always happening. If it's nothing else, the old turkey gobbler chases me around the tree." Don and Grandma laughed heartily, and Joyce joined in.

Grandma had promised to make some cookies this morning; so with Joyce on one side of her and Don on the other, she mixed up the dough and rolled it out on the large board. Then she got some cutters from the pantry, and cut out the cookies in all sorts of shapes. There were different kinds of animals, a bird for Joyce, and a queer little man for Don. His eyes, nose, and mouth were made out of raisins; also the buttons on his vest. Then she put the cookies in the oven to bake.

When they were done and Grandma took them out, Joyce's bird stuck to the pan and its tail came off. And Don's man had grown so fat that he had burst one of the buttons off his vest.

A long time ago, when the children's mother had been Grandma's little girl, she had lived on this very farm. In those far-off days she had planted a lilac bush and a cluster of prickly pear. Grandpa did not like the prickly pear, but he had let it grow all these years because his little girl had planted it.

"Isn't the grass nice and soft here?" said Don. "It feels

just like a velvet carpet. Watch me turn somersaults on it."

With that, he began to turn somersaults, going in the direction of the prickly pear. Joyce called to him to be careful, but it was too late; he came down right in the middle of the cactus plant. The long thorns pierced him like sharp needles; and although he tried to be brave, he could not keep back the tears.

There was nothing to do but to pull out the thorns one by one, and it took Grandma quite a while to do that. And although Don turned many somersaults afterward, he was always careful to keep away from the prickly pear.

When the story time came, Grandma, gently rocking back and forth, began: "I shall tell you tonight about a bee that it is very necessary to have in the home; and it is also much needed by those who have anything to do with animals. Its name is Bee Gentle. Have you ever noticed how gentle Grandpa is with all his animals?"

"Yes, I have noticed it," said Joyce. "And the horses love him for it, too. Whenever he goes to the pasture, they trot up to him and begin to nose about his pockets."

"He usually carries something in his pockets to give them," said Grandma. "He has raised all his horses from little colts; and he has always treated them kindly. Some men think they must treat animals roughly, to make them obey; but that is not so.

"Jake and Jenny were a brother and sister who loved each other dearly, but they were quite different in disposition. All the animals about the place were afraid of Jake, for he treated them roughly, and sometimes beat them. But they loved Jennie, because she was gentle with them. The dog would follow her about, and the cat would curl up on her lap and purr itself to sleep. When she went to the pasture, the horses would trot up to her and rub their noses on her shoulder. She often gave them lumps of sugar, or other dainties that horses like. No matter how wild or shy they were with others, Jenny could always catch them easily.

"Of all the horses in her father's pasture, Jenny loved best a beautiful swiftfooted mare called Fanny. Sometimes she would ride about the country on Fanny's back. But as gentle as the mare was with Jenny, she was afraid of Jake and would not let him catch her in the pasture.

" 'It would be much better,' Jenny would often say to her brother, 'if you would not treat the animals so roughly. See how easily I can handle Fanny— just because I am always gentle with her.'

" 'Oh,' Jake would answer with a laugh, 'that is all right for a woman, Jenny; but a man, you know, must show his authority.'

"Very early one morning, Jake's father came into his room. 'Jake,' he said, shaking the boy, 'wake up, son! Mother was taken very ill in the night. Catch Fanny and go for the doctor as quickly as you can.'

"The hired man was sleeping in the next room, and he heard what Jake's father said. He also got up and dressed, and hurried out to the pasture to help Jake catch the mare.

"The two were gone quite a while. At last they came back to the house, and Jake said, 'I can't catch Fanny, Father. She has jumped the ditch a dozen times. What shall I do?'

" 'Try again,' said his father. 'I can't leave Mother long enough to go to the pasture; and she must have help soon.'

"Just then Jenny came in. 'I will catch Fanny for you, Father,' she said, and hurried out to the pasture.

" 'Fanny, O Fanny!' she called; and the beautiful creature turned her head and trotted toward her. But an instant later, to Jenny's surprise, she galloped away across the field. Glancing behind her, Jenny saw Jake and the hired man coming up the lane.

" 'She sees you coming,' called Jenny; 'that's why she won't let me catch her. Go back to the house and wait; I'll bring her to you.'

"Jake and the man went back; and Jenny went farther into the pasture, calling, 'Fanny, O Fanny!' Instantly the mare turned and trotted toward her. She came close; and when Jenny gave her a lump of sugar, she rubbed her nose against the little girl's shoulder.

"Quickly she put the bridle on the mare, and led her through the lane to the barn. Then she harnessed her and hitched her to the buggy, and called to Jake. The boy hurried out, looking rather pale and worried; and as he stepped into the buggy Jenny stroked the mare's neck, saying gently, 'Now go along, dear Fanny, and do your best for Mother.'

"Fanny rubbed her nose against Jenny's shoulder again, as if to say, 'I will, little mistress; you may depend on me.' Then as Jake lifted the reins, she trotted down the road at a rapid gait.

"Jake found the doctor just sitting down to breakfast. When he heard the boy's story, he did not stop to eat. He rode right back with Jake, and in a short time he was at the mother's bedside. She was indeed very ill. 'If I had been a little later,' said the doctor in a low tone, 'I could have done nothing for her at all.'

"When Jake heard that, he went into the kitchen, sank down on a chair, and leaning his head on the table, he sobbed like a child. Jenny found him there a little later.

"She stood there beside him, gently stroking his hair. 'Jake,' she said at last, very softly, 'don't cry anymore, because God was very kind to us and didn't let it happen. But just think what might have been, if I hadn't been able to catch Fanny this morning. Don't you think it would pay to be always kind to the animals?'

"Jake nodded; he could not trust himself to speak.

"The sting of little Bee Gentle went very deep. Never again was Jake cruel to animals. He tried hard to make friends with Fanny; but she would have nothing to do with him. She remembered how roughly he had treated her in the past; and being only a horse, she did not understand that he never would do so again."

"How glad Jenny must have been," said Joyce, "that she had treated Fanny kindly! Because Fanny brought the doctor, and the doctor saved her mother's life."

"And besides," added Grandma softly, "people are always glad when they know they have done right."

Grandpa Could
Really Rope Them

"WHAT are you going to do with that rope?" asked Don, as Grandpa came from the shed with a coil of rope on his arm.

"Come with me, and you will find out," answered Grandpa. "And you may call Joyce, too, if you wish."

Don ran to the house to get Joyce, and soon the two came back together. They followed Grandpa down the lane toward the pasture where he kept his pigs. The children kept asking him what he intended to do, but he would only answer, "Wait and see."

Grandpa had a good many grown hogs, and ten little pigs. He opened the pasture gate and called to them, and they all came out into the lane, grunting and squealing. Then he coaxed them toward the pig-pen that he had been building. He closed the gate, and turning to the children said, "Now if you watch me, you will see what I intend to do with the rope."

When the children were both safe on the other side of the fence, Grandpa climbed into the pig-pen and coiled the rope a number of times in his hands. Then he cast it from him, and it fell over one of the little pigs. He drew it in, and the pig was caught. Then he lifted him and placed him in the pen. How the little fellow squealed, and how hard the old hogs tried to get to him! Some of the larger ones started toward the fence where Don and Joyce were perched on posts. Grandpa laughed to see how quickly the children scrambled down.

"Now," said Grandpa, "you see why I wanted the fence between you and those hogs, don't you? If they could get to you, they might tear you in pieces; for they want to take care of the little pigs."

Grandpa coiled the rope again and caught another of the little pigs, and then another and another, until all ten of them were in the pen. Then he opened the gate and turned the others back into the pasture.

Grandpa had caught the pigs so easily—only once or twice had he had to try a second time. "I don't see how you could catch them when they were running away from you," said Don. "I couldn't catch them if they were standing still."

"Perhaps not," said Grandpa. "But I can catch you if you try to get away from me. Just try it."

At that, Don began to run as fast as he could; but he had not gone far when he felt the rope slip over his shoulders, and he was lifted off his feet.

"What fun!" shouted Joyce. "Now try it on me."

Grandpa spent quite a while catching first one and then the other. Joyce was the hardest to catch, for after a few times she learned how to dodge the rope.

"Why did you put those little pigs in the pen?" asked Don, following close at his heels.

"They are getting in the cornfield," answered Grandpa, "and eating too much of my corn."

"But can't you keep them out?" asked Don.

"No," said Grandpa; "for when I mend one place in the fence, the little pigs are sure to find another place big enough to squeeze through. So the only way I can keep them out is to pen them up. Don, you may carry water for the little pigs—and they will need plenty, too, because it is so warm."

That pleased Don, and he began at once to fill the trough which Grandpa had placed in the pen.

That evening, Grandpa and Grandma and the children sat on the porch, listening to the chirp of the katydids and the call of the whippoorwills.

"Grandma," said Don, "what kind of bee will you

tell us about tonight?"

"Bee Sleepy, and go to bed," said Grandpa, with a wink at Grandma.

The children laughed. "No," said Don, "I don't want to hear about that bee—not yet."

"All right," said Grandma, "we'll have our story first; but we must begin right away, because it is almost bedtime. The bee I am thinking about tonight comes often to us all—especially to little children.

"Once there was a boy named Alfred who was the only child in his home. He was very selfish; and often he was determined to have his own way. But he had his good points, too.

"Alfred lived in the country; and during the Christmas holidays, he visited a friend of his who lived in the city. Then his friend in turn visited him during the summer vacation.

"As soon as his company came, Alfred thought it was quite too much for his mother to ask him to help her. He forgot how very ill she had been, and how frail she still was. Indeed, it was hard for him to think of anything but having a good time with his friend.

"The two boys had planned to spend a certain day at the creek, fishing. Of course they were eager to start as early as they could that morning. After they had gathered everything that they needed for their trip, they went out to the kitchen and found Alfred's mother packing a lunch for them.

" 'Alfred,' she said, 'I wish you would help me a little with the work before you go. I am afraid I shall not be able to do it all alone. Would you mind stopping long enough to wash the dishes and clean up the kitchen for me?'

"Alfred began to pout, but his mother continued, 'I

really wish you were not going fishing today. Your father will be away all day; and I would rather not be left alone, for I do not feel as well as usual. But I will not keep you, if you will wash the dishes before you go.'

"'Now, Mother,' said Alfred angrily, 'why do you ask me to do that, when you know I want to get started early? If I have to wait half the day, I don't care to go at all.'

"Just then the bee began to buzz about Alfred's ears. 'Help your mother! Help your mother!' it said. But Alfred did not pay any attention. 'Let the dishes go,' he cried. 'I don't care whether they are ever washed or not.' And picking up the lunch which his mother had packed so nicely for him, he started toward the creek. He did not even look back to say 'good-bye.'

"The boys found fishing very good that day. They caught a fine string of trout, ate their lunch, and in the middle of the afternoon were ready to start for home. Alfred was much pleased with their catch, and on the way home he said over and over, 'Won't Mother be glad we went fishing today, when she sees our string of trout? She is so fond of trout.' But even while he was saying it, he could not forget the tired look on his mother's face, or the hurt look in her eyes when he had refused to wash the dishes for her.

"When the boys reached the house, it seemed strangely quiet. They found the dishes cleared away, and the kitchen neatly swept. Alfred's mother was lying on the couch, and she seemed to be resting very comfortably.

" 'See, Mother,' said Alfred, 'isn't this a nice string of trout?'

"But Mother did not answer. Alfred spoke to her again. Still no answer. He touched her hand then, and found it icy-cold.

"Then the awful truth dawned upon him—his mother was dead! She had died while he was fishing; but she had done the work that she had asked her boy to do.

"All his life, poor Alfred felt the sting of the bee that had buzzed about him on that summer morning. What hurt him most deeply was that he would never again have a chance to help his frail little mother who had done so much for him."

"I'm so glad," said Joyce, "that I still have my mother, and that I can do things for her when she is tired."

"It's a sad story, Grandma," said little Don, "but I'm glad you told it to us. I'm going to remember it always."

The Tree With

A Strange Knot

GRANDMA HAD GOTTEN UP EARLY—in fact, it was long before Don or Joyce awakened. She usually went to the garden where she would hoe the vegetables and then would spend some time in prayer and meditation. Everyone knew that she loved the freshness of the early morning, and the opportunity to be alone.

This morning Joyce had awakened much earlier than usual and decided that she would go down to the garden. Maybe she could help grandmother pick the peas she had mentioned the day before.

As Joyce slipped by Don's room she saw he was still asleep, so she tip-toed softly down the stairs. He was a real sleepy head and . . . well, she and grandma would get the work done before breakfast she imagined.

When Joyce reached the garden she found Grandma sitting on a bench singing. The peas were already picked and she was shelling them.

"Goodmorning, Grandma," Joyce spoke cheerfully. "Please, may I help you? I couldn't sleep, so I thought I would help you in the garden—but I see you're almost through!"

"Well, Joyce, I appreciate your thoughtfulness," Grandma smiled as she moved over to make room on the bench for Joyce. "You are so very much like your mother when she was your age. I recall how many mornings she would be out here helping me, but more than that I remember the wonderful times we had talking together. But . . . that is at least thirty years ago. I missed her so much when she left."

Joyce loved to hear Grandma tell the many funny things her mother did when she was a little girl. "Grandma," she asked, "was this same bench here then? And this garden? And this gate?"

"Yes, Joyce," Grandma replied thoughtfully. "When your mother was little and came out to help me, we often sat on this same bench. The garden didn't have a fence around it then, so the gate was not here until about ten years ago."

Grandma looked up as she continued speaking, "And this big tree we're sitting under was just a little sapling. In fact, all these large trees were planted in a straight row near the garden when your mother started school. Now they are wonderful shade trees. And see that third tree over there—the one with the gnarled trunk? I must tell you how that happened."

As the two walked toward the tree Grandma continued, "In those days we had a neighbor boy who loved to come over and play with your mother. They spent many hours playing in the garden. Well, he always loved to tie knots in whatever he could find; and one day he tied a knot in this tree! At that time it was just a small sapling and was tender and could be easily bent. He just twisted it under and around and made a neat little knot! Of course

when he did this the little tree was no thicker than my little finger, but now, as you see, it is about six inches through!"

"Oh! what a strange way for a tree to grow," exclaimed Joyce as she ran her hands over the gnarled trunk with its unusual knot.

"Yes," Grandma replied. "You see we didn't know that Harry had twisted the little sapling into a knot for . . . oh, I suppose it was more than a year later and of course it was then too late. When Grandpa found it he decided it could not be untied. And really it has been a good lesson to all of us ever since.

"You know, Joyce, there is an old saying, 'As the twig is bent so it will grow.' This means that as boys and girls are bent when they are young, so they will grow! The way you start out in life—the habits you develop when you are young, will determine what you will be like when you grow up."

"Oh, that is interesting," Joyce thoughtfully agreed. "And to think the knot is still here after these thirty years."

A few minutes later they were at the breakfast table. Joyce was eager for Don to see the tree. She explained all about it as they ate.

In his typical manner Grandpa added, "At first I was put out with the children when I found the tree in a knot. But I guess it has served a useful purpose. All through the years we have called it our lesson tree. It has been a good reminder to all of us how impossible it is to undo some things!"

Don could hardly wait to finish his breakfast. He wanted to see that strange knot in the tree which had its beginning years before when his mother was just a little girl.

So it was that Don and Joyce played by the tree all morning. Don imagined that he was in a lookout post as he climbed to the tallest branch. And then in the afternoon they carried lunch to Grandpa down in the meadow where he was cutting hay. They had never seen a sickle bar cut the swath of hay and lay it so evenly.

After they had finished supper they hastened to the porch to enjoy the cool of the evening. It had been a very warm day and they enjoyed the gentle breeze that was blowing.

"Now is it time for our story, Grandma?" Joyce asked expectantly. "What Bee do we learn about tonight?"

"Well," said Grandma as she made herself comfortable on the porch swing, "I want us to discover the importance of heeding another Bee—a Bee which can save us from lots of difficulty if we learn to mind its buzzing. Its name is BEE CAREFUL.

"This morning you have both seen that knot in the

tree. Because two children were careless and left the little sapling twisted in a knot, now 30 years later we have that ugly gnarl to mar the beauty of the tree.

"Now I want to tell you about the Brown family. There were three children: Susan, Bobby and Teddy. One evening when Mr. Brown arrived home from work he found his little daughter, Susan, sitting on the front steps. By the expression on her face he could tell that she seemed quite unhappy. He sat down beside her.

" 'Tell me, my little Gumdrop (that was his pet name for her) what is all the scowling about? Have you been fussing with your brothers again?' "

"Susan heaved a heavy sigh. 'Oh, Daddy, why do I continue to do awful things that aggravate others and make them angry at me?'

" 'What awful things?'

" 'Oh . . . you know I . . . I just talk too much . . . even when I know it will hurt others. But I can't seem to keep still. I know it isn't kind and folk get upset with the things I often say, which are really none of my business.'

" 'You do talk pretty much,' " agreed her father, " 'but why does that make you sad just now?'

" 'Well, Daddy, things have gone bad all day. This morning I guess I was jealous because Bobby had gotten a better report card than I, so I told Mother that yesterday he had forgotten to leave the note with Grandma until after school. It was a note she wanted delivered before school. I guess I shouldn't have tattled, even though it was the truth. So Bobby told my friends at school that I was a blabber-mouth sister. They all laughed at me and now they call me blabber-mouth when I talk! Oh, why do I talk so much?' There were tears in Susan's eyes as she looked up at her Daddy.

" 'Well, I see you do have a problem. Could I help?' he asked gently.

" 'But Daddy, that isn't all! A little while ago Bobby and his friend Sam were getting ready to go on a hike. I told Sam I was surprised that he wanted to go hiking with Bobby for I had heard Bobby complained how slowly he walked and how he spoiled their last hike. Well, that caused Sam to get angry at Bobby and he went home—so their hike was off. Now Bobby won't speak to me. None of this was really any of my business!' "

Grandma looked right at Joyce as she asked, "What do you suppose that Father did to help Susan? He knew that Susan was sorry for her careless talking and the unnecessary tattling that made discord between friends. He also knew she must learn to listen to the buzzing of the Bee telling her to BEE CAREFUL how she used her tongue.

"As Susan had been talking, her father thought of a way to teach her a most important lesson. He reached over to the lawn by his side and picked a dandelion which was white with fluffy seeds.

" 'Here, Susan, blow hard on this dandelion. See how far you can blow these seeds into the air,' he said handing the dandelion to her.

"Susan took a deep breath and gave a hard blow that sent the fluffy seeds in all directions. For a few moments they watched the seeds float away in the breeze.

" 'Now, Susan, I would like to have you gather all those seeds together and put them in my hand! I'll just sit here and wait.'

"Susan looked to see if he was joking. She could hardly believe that he meant it. 'But Daddy, she cried, 'I . . . I couldn't possibly gather those dandelion seeds together

again. Why! I can't even see them or find them.'

" 'You see, Susan,' her father said gently, 'anyone can scatter such seeds with a little careless puff of breath. But the wisest, most earnest man cannot gather them up again. Just so unkind, careless talking goes on and on spoiling and hindering friendships—hurting people. It is impossible to gather up or undo words that have been spoken. They will continue to leave their scar—or form a 'knot' in someone's thinking.'

" 'Isn't there something I can do to show my brothers I'm sorry and want to be a different sister. One that is kind and thoughtful,' she sobbed.

" 'Yes there is,' her father agreed, ' I believe there is something you can do, but I'll let you decide what it is!' He left her to think it through.

"Sometime later the Brown family gathered for the evening meal. Just before they bowed their heads to give thanks for their food Susan asked, 'Daddy, first may I tell Teddy that I'm sorry for my jealous and hateful tattling,' and looking at Bobby she asked, 'Will you forgive me for my careless words and sowing discord between you and Sam?'

"Both of her brothers were ready to forgive her when they saw she was really sincere. Father prayed that Susan and all the members of the family would learn a lesson through her sad experiences and that the Lord would set a guard over their mouth and a watch over the door of their lips. Psalm 141:3."

There was a long pause as Grandma finished her story. Finally she said, "I'm quite sure that from that time Susan was quick to hear the Bee Careful buzzing when she was tempted to share some careless words."

Joyce and Don were giving each other a knowing nod as they went off to bed.

A Horse

Rang The Bell

That Day

ANOTHER morning came to the farm—another day for the children to roam about the fields and enjoy themselves in God's big, free out-of-doors. How much more pleasant than having to play in their own yard in the city, these hot summer days!

In that long-ago time when the children's mother had lived on the farm, Grandpa had given her a pony of her own to drive to school in the village. Old Ned was still on the place. Grandpa was always ready to saddle and bridle him, whenever the children wished to go for a ride.

Today, as the children wandered to the back of the orchard, wishing for something to do, Ned stood on the other side of the fence and neighed at them. That gave Don an idea.

"O Joyce!" he cried, "let's ride Ned around in the pasture."

"Without a saddle?" exclaimed Joyce.

"Of course," answered Don in his most grown-up tone; "why not?"

"All right," said Joyce a little doubtfully."

They went out through the barn lot, leaving the gate open behind them. Then, letting down the bars, they soon found themselves in the pasture.

Joyce led old Ned to the fence, holding to his mane. She climbed up on the fence, and then on to the horse's back. Don quickly climbed on behind her.

In his younger days, Ned had been taught a number of tricks, which he still remembered. He would shake hands, and nod his head, and ride up steps. And when a rider was on his back, if he gripped his knees in Ned's sides, the old horse would gallop away as fast as he could.

Always, before this, the children had ridden with a saddle; and so they had never had to hold fast with their knees. But today Joyce knew she would have to hold on tightly, so she pressed her knees hard against old Ned's sides. Instantly he started to gallop across the pasture. He went up the lane, through the open gate into the barn lot, and on to the watering trough. Joyce still held to his mane with all her might, gripping him tightly with her knees. Don bounced up and down behind her, with his arms about her waist.

When Ned reached the watering trough, he stopped. Suddenly he lowered his head, and both children slipped off into the trough. It was about half-full of water, and Joyce fell in face downward. Such sputtering, puffing, and blowing, as they scrambled out of the trough! And

there stood old Ned, looking at them as if to say, "How did you like your bath?"

Grandpa came hurrying up to see if they were hurt. He told them that old Ned was only doing as he had been taught when he was a colt; and that they could not expect him to do otherwise, if they rode him like that.

That evening, as twilight settled down, Grandpa and Grandma and the children sat on the porch and listened to the lonely call of a whippoorwill from the neighboring woods.

"I see the Big Bear," said Don—"and the Little Bear, too."

"What is the Milky Way, Grandma?" asked Joyce.

"When men look through telescopes they find millions of stars—so close together and so far away that not one star can be seen by the naked eye. The Indians used to say it was the path which all Indians must travel after they died, to reach the Happy Hunting Grounds."

"See how bright the stars are in the Dipper!" exclaimed Don.

"When I was just a little girl," said Grandma, "I learned a rhyme about the Milky Way:

"The Man in the Moon that sails through the sky
Is known as a gay old skipper.
But he made a mistake,
When he tried to take
A drink of milk from the dipper.
He dipped it into the Milky Way,
And was just prepared to drink it,
When the Big Bear growled,
And the Little Bear growled,
And it scared him so that he spilled it."

The children liked the queer little rhyme, and said it over until they knew it by heart.

At last Grandpa said, "I guess it's about time to turn in for tonight."

"Oh, no," said Don—"not till Grandma tells us a story."

"All right," said Grandma; "I shall tell you this time about a little bee called Bee Grateful. It has a very sharp sting, as you will see.

"Far way, under sunny Italian skies, there is an old, old town by the name of Atri. It is built on the side of a steep hill.

"A very long time ago, the king of Atri bought a great golden-toned bell and hung it in the tower at the market-place. Fastened to the bell, there was a long rope that reached almost to the ground.

" 'We shall call it the bell of justice,' said the king.

"He proclaimed a great holiday in Atri, and invited everyone to come to the market-place and see the bell. It shone like gold in the bright sunlight. When the king came riding down the street, the people whispered to one another, 'Perhaps he will ring the bell.'

"But he did not. Instead, he stopped at the foot of the tower and raised his hand. All the whispering and talking stopped; for the people knew that the king was about to speak.

" 'My good people,' he said, 'this bell belongs to you. No one must ever pull the rope unless he is in trouble. But if any one of you—man, woman, or child—is ever treated unjustly, you may come to the market-place and ring the bell. The judges will come together and listen to your story; and the one who has done wrong will be punished, whoever he may be. That is why this is called the bell of justice.'

"Year after year passed by, and the great bell still hung in the tower. Many people who were in trouble had rung the bell; and in every case, the judges had been perfectly fair, and had punished the one who had done wrong.

"The rope had hung there so long in the sun and rain, and had been pulled by so many hands, that it was almost worn out. Some of the strands were untwisted; and it had grown shorter and shorter, until only the tallest man or woman could reach it.

" 'We must have a new rope,' said the judges at last. 'If a little child should be wronged, he could not reach high enough to ring the bell. That would never do.'

"At once the people of Atri set about to look for a new rope; but there was none to be found in all the town of Atri. They would have to send someone to a country across the mountains to get the rope. But that would take quite a while; and what should they do, while they were waiting?

"One man thought of a plan. He ran to his vineyard and came back with a grapevine. Then he tied the vine to the rope.

"'There!' he said, 'the smallest child will be able to reach it now, and ring the bell'; for the vine, with its leaves and little tendrils, trailed on the ground.

"'The judges were pleased. 'Yes,' they said, 'that will do very well, until we can get a new rope from the country beyond the mountains.'

"Near the village of Atri, higher up on the hillside, there lived an old soldier. When he was a young man, he had traveled in far-distant countries, and had fought in

many wars. And he was so brave that his king had made him a knight.

"He had had one true and faithful friend all through those hard and dangerous years. It was his horse. Many a time the brave steed had saved his master's life.

"But now that the knight was an old man, he no longer wished to do brave deeds. He cared now for only one thing—gold, *gold*, GOLD. He was a miser.

"One day, as he passed his barn, he looked in and saw his faithful horse standing in his stall. The poor creature looked almost starved.

" 'Why should I keep that lazy beast any longer?' said the miser to himself. 'His food costs more money than he is worth. I know what I will do. I will turn him out on the hillside, and let him find his own food. If he starves to death—why, he will be out of the way!'

"So the brave old horse was turned out to graze as best he could on the rocky hillside. He was sick and lame, and he grew thinner every day; for all he could find was a tiny patch of grass or a thistle now and then. The village dogs barked at him and bit at his heels; and naughty boys threw stones at him.

"One hot afternoon, the old horse limped into the market-place of Atri. No one was about the streets; for the people were trying to keep as cool as they could in the shelter of their homes. As the horse went picking about trying to find a few blades of grass, suddenly he discovered the long grapevine trailing on the ground at the foot of the tower. The leaves were still green and tender, for it had been placed there only a short time before.

"The horse did not know that the bell would ring if he pulled the vine. He only knew that here was a juicy bit of dinner for him, and he was hungry.

"He nibbled at the end of the vine; and suddenly, far

up in the belfry, the huge bell began to swing back and forth. From its great throat, golden music floated down over the town of Atri. It seemed to be saying:

" 'Some — one —— has — done —— me — wrong!
Ding — dong —— ding — dong!'

"The judges put on their robes, and hurried out of their cool homes into the hot streets of the village. Who was in trouble, they wondered?

"When they reached the market-place, no one was

there; but they saw the starving old horse, nibbling at the tender grapevine.

" 'Ho, ho!' cried one, 'it is the miser's brave old steed. He rings the bell to plead for justice.'

" 'And justice he shall have!' cried another.

" 'See how thin he is,' said a lad with a kind heart.

"By this time, many people had gathered in the market-place. When they saw the old horse, a murmur of astonishment swept through the crowd.

" 'The miser's steed!' cried one to another. 'He has waited long; but he shall have justice today.'

" 'I have seen the old horse wandering on the hillside day after day, in search of food,' said an old man.

" 'And while the noble steed has no shelter,' said his neighbor, 'his master sits at home, counting his gold.'

" 'Bring his master to us!' cried the judges sternly.

"And so they brought him. In silence he waited to hear what the judges would say.

" 'This brave steed of yours,' they said, 'has served you faithfully for many a long year. He has saved your life in times of danger. He has helped you to hoard your bags of gold. Therefore, hear your sentence, O Miser! Half of your gold shall be taken from you, and used to buy food and shelter for your faithful horse.'

"The miser hung his head. It made him sad to lose his gold; but the people laughed and shouted, as the old horse was led away to a comfortable stall and a dinner fit for the steed of a king."

"Hooray!" cried Don. "Good for the brave old horse! Grandpa, I'm so glad you aren't a miser!" He was thinking of old Ned, with his sleek, shining black coat.

"Bedtime!" announced Grandma, as she led the way into the house. "Goodnight, children—and happy dreams to you!"

You Couldn't Help
But Love Her

WHEN the children ran down to meet the mailman in the morning, he handed them another letter from Mother. She and Daddy were going home next Friday, she said; and they must be there Saturday, to start school on the following Monday.

"Only three more nights to be here," said Joyce, taking the letter in to Grandma. "I want to go home and see Mother and Daddy, but I wish I could stay on the farm, too."

"And only three more stories about bees," added Don. "We must remember them all, Joyce, so we can tell them to Mother."

"What do you want to do today, children?" asked Grandma.

"After our morning work is done," said Joyce, with her most grown-up air, "we must finish weeding the flower-bed."

"Grandma," called Don a little later, "come and see how nice it looks where we pulled the weeds yesterday."

Grandma stood for a moment thoughtfully looking down at the half-weeded bed of flowers.

"Children," she asked suddenly, "If you wanted a flower this morning, where would you pick it—in the part of the bed that is full of weeds, or in that patch over there that you have weeded so nicely?"

"I would pick my flower where there aren't any weeds," answered Don, wondering why she asked. "I

would take that pretty big red one right over there."

"And so would I," declared Joyce, pulling up a stubborn weed.

"But why wouldn't you take this one?" asked Grandma, as she parted the weeds and showed another red beauty.

"Well," answered Don, "I s'pose it's just as pretty, but some way the weeds make it look ugly."

"That's just what I was thinking about," said Grandma. "I have seen children who were like this flower in the weeds. They had beautiful faces; but they let the weeds of disobedience, selfishness, deceit, and pride grow all about them; until you could not see their beauty for the ugly weeds.

"This garden makes me think of two cousins that I knew once. One was obedient, unselfish, and kind to everybody; and although she did not have a beautiful face, she was loved by all who knew her. The other girl had a beautiful face; but she had such an unlovely disposition that nobody cared for her, and so she was left very much to herself. Her beauty, like this lovely flower, was quite hidden by the ugly weeds growing all around her.

"These weeds in the flower-bed were very small in the beginning; but they grew and grew, until now they are taller than the flowers. And the weeds in God's child-gardens are small at first, too. To begin with, there springs up the weed of telling a story that is not quite true. If it is not pulled up at once, soon it grows up into a big ugly lie weed. Other weeds—disobedience, selfishness, and unkindness—spring up around it; and soon the beautiful flower is hidden by the tall weeds. And when the Master of the Garden wants a lovely flower-child to do a kind deed for Him, He never thinks of choosing one that is surrounded by weeds."

"What a nice story!" exclaimed Joyce. "But it wasn't about a bee, Grandma."

"Yes, it was," said Don—"Don't Bee Weedy."

"But there haven't been any Don't Bees in the stories before," said Joyce. "Besides, I wouldn't call that Don't Bee Weedy; I'd call it Bee Clean."

"That's a good name for it," said Grandma. "I hope you'll always keep your lives clean from the weeds that children so often allow to grow up around them."

Grandma went back to the house, while the children set to work weeding the rest of the flower-bed. They were very careful not to pull up any of the flowers with the weeds. When they had finished, the flower-bed looked beautiful, cleared as it was of all weeds and grasses.

"I surely don't want ugly weeds to grow in *my* garden, so I shall always listen to Bee Clean," said Joyce softly, as she walked slowly toward the house.

"Will you make us a kite, Grandpa?" asked Don after

dinner.

"Yes, do!" cried Joyce. "It will be such fun to fly it."

"Well," said Grandpa, "you children hunt around and find some sticks. Then ask Grandma for some paper and paste and string; and bring them out to the woodshed, and I'll try my hand at making a kite."

After it was made, they had to let it lie in the sun for a while, to dry. Then they took it out to the pasture. There was a soft breeze blowing, and Grandpa said the kite ought to fly. Don took the string and ran along with it for quite a distance. The wind lifted it a little; but after it had darted back and forth, it fell on the ground. This happened several times, and at last Grandpa said, "It's too bad, children, but my kite won't fly. But I'll see if I can make something else for you."

Then Grandpa took some thin boards and whittled out darts. He took a short stick, and tied a string to it; and then he fitted the string in a notch which he had cut in one end of the dart. He threw the dart up in the air, ever so high. It came down just a few yards from Don. The sharp end stuck fast; and there it stood, upright in the ground.

Don was as much pleased with this as he would have been with a kite that would fly. Soon he and Joyce were shooting darts into the air, to see whose would go the highest.

They had so much fun that the afternoon flew by very fast. It was nearly suppertime when Don gathered up the darts and took them to the house with him. He carefully put them away in the little trunk, saying, "I'll show the boys how to throw darts when I get home."

That evening, as they sat on the porch in the quiet twilight, they heard the faint tinkle of a cowbell in the distance. They talked a while, and then they sang some songs together.

"It's story time, isn't it?" said Grandpa by and by. "Who is going to get stung tonight?" he asked, winking at Joyce.

"I hope *I* don't," she laughed, remembering the time the bee had stung her on the first day of her visit.

"No one shall be stung tonight," said Grandma. "I have a very sweet little bee to tell you about. And because the little girl in my story listened to its buzz, it made honey for her all her life. Its name is Bee Loving; and it can do things that nothing else in the world can do. You know people can sometimes be *loved* into doing things that they could not be persuaded to do in any other way.

"Gene was a very little girl who had been left alone in the world. She had never seen her father; and her mother had died when she was only two and a half. Some kind people had taken care of the little girl when her mother was ill; and when she died, they tried to find her relatives, to ask what should be done with Gene. But they could not find any trace of them.

"When Gene was three, these kind people wanted to go away for a couple of weeks, and they asked a lady to take care of the child while they were gone. The lady was very glad to do this, for she loved little children. And so Gene came to stay in the big mansion where the lady, her husband, and grown-up daughter lived.

"The lady's husband did not like children very well, and it always annoyed him whenever little Gene came near him. She had a sunny disposition and a very sweet smile, and she tried to make friends with the man; but he would not pay any attention to her.

"He always read his paper in the morning before he went to work, and in the evening after he came home.

Little Gene would peep up at him under the paper, with her sweetest smile. He would lay the paper down, and walk away; but soon he would come back and pick it up and begin to read again. And in a moment, there little Gene would be, peeping up at him with her lovely smile.

"One day when Gene had been living in the home about a week, the man was reading his paper and she was peeping under it with her usual smile. Suddenly he laid aside the paper and took her in his arms. He kissed her on her forehead, saying tenderly, 'It doesn't matter how hard a man tries to keep from loving you; you just love your way right into his heart.'

"Gene threw her small arms about his neck, and laid her curly head on his shoulder, saying in her pretty baby way, 'Gene woves oo, big man.'

"That completely won his heart; and when the two weeks had passed and Gene's friends came after her, he did not want to give her up. So he decided to keep her and bring her up as if she had been his own little girl. This also pleased his wife and grown-up daughter very much, for they had loved little Gene from the beginning.

"Gene is grown now, but she still has the same sunny disposition and the same sweet smile, which make her beloved by all who know her. Nothing but love could have won for her the beautiful home she has had all these years. And to this day, Bee Loving is still helping her to win her way through life. The greatest victories are always those that are won through love."

"I know someone that I love," said little Don, throwing his arms round Grandma's neck.

"So do I," said Joyce as she kissed Grandma good-night.

The Strangest

Lamb

SUNDAY MORNING Don sat with Grandpa in the front seat of the car as they waited. In a few minutes Joyce and Grandma got in the back seat and they were off to the little white church across the valley just a few miles away.

Of course Don and Joyce looked forward to Sunday for they could dress up in their best clothes and they also got to see their friends. But most of all they looked forward to the special story the minister always told the boys and girls.

It was a lovely morning as they drove along the country roads. As they reached the church they could see many friends and neighbors had already arrived.

Soon they were singing. How Don and Joyce loved to sing the lovely hymns. The pastor prayed and then it was time for the special story. As he stepped down in front of the children he said: "Today I want to tell you about a friend of mine when I lived back in Scotland before moving to this country. One day my friend, who was a minister, was teaching a small boy in the home of one of his members to read the twenty-third Psalm.

"The little boy began reading, 'The Lord is my Shepherd.'

"The old minister interrupted him to say, 'No, no, you don't read it right!'

"Again the little boy began. Slowly and earnestly he read, 'The Lord is my shepherd.'

" 'No, you don't read it right yet,' said the old minister. 'Now watch me.' The minister held up his left hand.

He placed the forefinger of his right hand on the thumb of the left hand and said, 'The!' Then he placed the forefinger of the right hand on the next finger and said, 'Lord!' Then, he placed it on the third finger and said, 'Is!' And then, grasping hold of the fourth finger on his left hand, he said 'MY!' 'You see Son, you take hold of that fourth finger and say MY!'

" 'Oh,' cried the little boy: 'now I see it . . . it's the Lord is MY Shepherd. Now I understand what you mean!'

"You know, boys and girls," the minister continued, "the Bible explains that we are all like sheep who have wanted our own way. So we have all gone astray. Those who grow older and still follow their own selfish ways find it harder and harder to yield to Jesus as their Lord and Shepherd. Sometimes folk go on for years and years while the Shepherd is seeking for His lost sheep. He calls and calls but they do not seem to hear. They go on as sheep without a shepherd.

"Several years ago when I was visiting in the Bible Land a friend and I went out to talk to one of the shepherds who care for the sheep. That evening we observed how carefully the shepherd watched his sheep enter the fold. He stood counting each one as they passed into the fold.

"When the last one had entered, my friend asked him, 'Now that you have them all in for the night, where is the door?'

"The shepherd smiled and then replied, 'I am the door!' And then to show us, he lay down across the opening to the sheepfold! Nothing could pass in or out of the fold without going over his body.

"You see, boys and girls," the pastor said earnestly, "when we receive Jesus as our Lord, He becomes our Shepherd and Savior. He accepts us into His fold and from that time on we know His voice and enjoy His protection.

"If you have never before told Him that you want to turn from living for yourself and you want to receive Him as your Lord, why not do it just now as we bow our hearts together?"

After he prayed for each boy and girl he went on to give his morning message to the entire congregation. Following this everyone went home.

Joyce could hardly wait until they got in the car so she could tell them something very special. Finally they were on their way home.

"Oh Grandma and Grandpa," she spoke happily. "That was such an interesting lesson about the sheep and the shepherd. You know, right as the pastor prayed for us I told Jesus that I was sorry I had been going my own way. I told Him I did want to receive Him as my Lord and my Shepherd, and I know that right then He accepted me into His fold. Oh, I'm so happy for now I know that I belong to Him. He is MY Shepherd!"

"Joyce, we are happy to hear you say this. Both Grandpa and I can remember when we were about your age and *we* were accepted into God's fold."

The afternoon slipped by so fast. Soon it was evening and they were sitting on the porch. Grandpa turned to Don, "I guess maybe we have a homesick boy . . . is that right Don? All afternoon we have noticed a cloud hanging over you."

"Well . . . I guess . . . well, it would be nice to see Mother and Daddy. It really won't be long now before we will be going back home. But really, I've been thinking about what the minister said this morning, and about what Joyce told us in the car.

"Grandpa, I guess . . . maybe that's what is wrong with me. I am still a sheep outside the fold." Big tears were welling up in his eyes.

Grandma spoke gently, "Yes, Don, all of us must realize that we are like sheep gone astray and we need a Shepherd. Next, all we need to do is tell Him that we want to receive Him as our Lord, and He will accept us."

"That's right Don," Joyce added, "The Lord Jesus is waiting to receive us into His fold."

"Don," Grandma asked, "would you like to tell the Lord right now?"

"Oh yes!" Don's face flushed with more tears.

So they all bowed their heads together as Don prayed. Then Joyce thanked the Lord for accepting her and for accepting Don too. Next Grandma prayed and then Grandpa thanked the Lord that He would be their faithful Shepherd all through the years.

When Grandpa was through praying, Don took one big leap into his lap. "My boy, I'm so glad the burden and

cloud has now lifted. And you know that you have received Jesus as your Lord and He has now accepted you into His fold. From now on you, too, can say, 'The Lord is MY Shepherd.' "

Grandma put her arms around Joyce as she spoke, "I'm so glad that both of you have given yourselves to the Lord while you are very young. How wonderful to have a full life to give to Him.

"The story I had selected for tonight will mean much more to each of you now. The name of this Bee we shall call BEE ACCEPTED. I think I will read it to you!

DR. WALTER WILSON TELLS of driving through the countryside one day with a friend. As they passed a meadow with a flock of grazing sheep, they saw a little lamb playing by its mother.

"Look at that lamb," Dr. Wilson exclaimed. "Did

you ever see a lamb that looked like it was 'wearing' its fleece! As they talked they decided to stop and visit with the farmer who stood nearby working on a fence.

While talking, they asked him about the lamb. He laughed and explained. "Yes, there is an interesting story behind that little fellow you see out there with his mother. Earlier this spring when a little lamb was born, its mother died and it became an orphan. If you have ever tried to bottlefeed a little lamb, you know how difficult it is to care for a hungry, unprotected orphan.

"Well, about that same time another sheep had a lamb that died at birth. I found her lamb lying cold and still in a shed. I supposed that mother was out in the field wondering what had become of her lamb.

"Suddenly, it occurred to me that I might get that mother to accept the little orphan lamb! So I decided to put the mother sheep in a pen. A little later I put the orphan lamb in the pen with her hoping she would accept it as her own.

"At first she paid no attention to it, but finally with some pushing and pulling, I got her to the side of the little lamb. But what do you think she did? She took one smell of the poor little thing and then began to butt it this way and that! I immediately rescued the lamb realizing she would not accept it as her own!

"Of course I was disappointed. How could I get her to accept this little orphan? Well, I decided to try something else. I went over to the shed and got her own lamb and brought it to her pen. Instantly, there was a calm; she smelled the lamb and knew it was her own.

"You would have said that lamb was no different from any other in the flock, but the mother knew better! She recognized it as her own, and the only one in all the world that could satisfy her mother-heart.

"Well, after several hours of leaving the dead lamb by her side, I took it to another shed where I skinned it. Then I took that skin and securely tied it around the body of the little orphan lamb!

"Back to the pen I went with the little orphan, who was wearing the skin of another! What do you think that mother sheep did now? Well, she looked closely at the lamb for a moment, smelled it carefully and seemed to recognize the smell as belonging to her own lamb. Strange as it may seem, she was now ready to accept the little orphan as her own, and in just a few moments the little lamb was happily nursing."

As the farmer looked at Dr. Wilson and his friend he smiled and continued to say, "Yes, that little lamb that looks so strange is 'wearing' his fleece—the fleece of another. But because he is, he has been accepted by a mother

other than his own. I guess I really could take that fleece off anytime now, but I have wanted to be very sure she had completely accepted the little fellow."

Dr. Wilson and his friend thanked the farmer for telling them about the little orphan lamb and they drove away.

Grandma finished reading. She continued, "you know this story of the little lamb describes our condition before we were accepted into God's family. You see all of us have been much like little orphan lambs who were outside the fold. The only way we can be accepted into the fold of God's family is by wearing the 'royal fleece' which Jesus provided when He died on Calvary.

"Of course we must not imagine that we can trick or fool God. No, it is just that God is holy and cannot accept us while we are still in our sin. So when we ask forgiveness for all the wrong we have done, then God sees us wearing Christ's robe of righteousness, or as we have called it, the royal fleece.

"Nor does this mean that we can do what we like afterward. The Lord Jesus not only gives us His robe of righteousness, but He also sends His Spirit to live in us to help us live acceptable unto God. So you see, Don and Joyce, first we are 'accepted in the Beloved Son,' and then by the help of God's Spirit we are able to 'live acceptable unto God.'

"And that is where we differ from the poor little orphan lamb of our story. He wears his covering only a few weeks or maybe months, until his mother gets used to him. We, however, have our robe to wear forever, and our Inner Helper to be with us forever. Isn't that wonderful?"

"And now little lambs," Grandpa said gently, "you must hasten along to your beds. See you in the morning."

Protected

From Danger

DURING THE NIGHT it began to storm. How the wind did blow—it blew with such force it shook the whole house! Then it began to rain; soon it hailed. Don and Joyce woke up as Grandpa moved about closing windows in their rooms.

"I'm afraid!" called Don. "And so am I!" echoed Joyce as they ran for Grandma's room.

In a few moments Grandma was explaining to them that the weather conditions had been just right all evening for a storm front to pass over.

"But you know children," she continued, "since we are God's sheep in His fold, we can ask the Lord to protect us—in fact, we can be sure that He will watch over us as we trust Him." So they each prayed and then Grandma tucked them into bed again.

But a few minutes later the wind seemed to increase; the rain beat hard against the windows and they rattled even more. Then there was a terrible C-R-A-S-H . . . !

"What was that?" shouted Don as he sat straight up in bed!

Immediately Grandpa was in Don's room looking out of the window. As a sudden flash of lightening lit up the whole yard Grandpa could see what had caused the loud noise. "Don," he said turning from the window, "our big maple tree has just fallen! But don't be afraid. I believe the storm has almost passed over and soon all will be quiet again. In the morning we can find out what the storm has done."

Sure enough, just as Grandpa had promised, in a few minutes the storm was over; everything was quiet. They all went back to sleep again.

Next morning as Don and Joyce came down the stairs Grandpa looked up to say, "Good morning children. I'll be really glad for my helpers today! After last night's storm we have a big, big job. The wind has broken and scattered branches all over the yard. Come! Before we eat, let me show you how the big maple has just missed the house!

As they walked out into the yard, Grandpa pointed to the shattered trunk. "We had no idea the inside was so rotten, though I might have suspected it by several dead branches that were in the top of the tree."

Grandma sighed! "It is a real marvel that the tree missed the house."

"But Grandma! We prayed," interrupted Don.

"That's right Don, and I'm sure the Lord answered our prayers by keeping the tree from crashing down on

the roof. The direction of the wind last night should have sent this tree right down on the house, but instead, it is just as though a Hand had pushed it another direction. And you see the only damage was to the side of the garage."

"Oh! I'm glad we are *in His fold*," Joyce confided.

Soon they were gathered at the breakfast table and Grandpa thanked the Lord for His protection and for directing the tree away from the house where it would surely have fallen on Don's room. As they were eating, it was evident Don was thinking. You could almost see the thoughts clouding his face. Finally he spoke.

"Grandpa, last night when it was storming you and Grandma were not afraid—at least not like I was! I guess it is because you know God is able to protect you. Well . . . why doesn't the Lord just keep it from storming and give us only nice weather—then He wouldn't have to turn the tree in the other direction when it falls."

Grandpa cleared his throat and paused . . . It was a big question, but he knew this inquiring young mind must have some kind of answer. He began, "You see Don, God is able to stop any storm that does not serve His higher purpose. But we must see that He allows storms for various reasons. First, you will see, when we start cleaning the yard, that the storm has pruned many dead twigs and branches from the trees; so nature is benefited by the storm.

"Second," Grandpa continued, "we also know God can use the storms to speak to people who are selfishly going their own way unconcerned about God's purpose for their life. I imagine that during every severe storm many people begin to pray and consider whether they are ready to meet God. But then for those of us who know Him as our Shepherd—and we know we are in His fold—it is God's way of developing our confidence in Him. You see how God's protection last night has given you new confidence. That word confidence really means *with faith.* So we are to learn to *live with faith.*"

"Say, Grandma," he said smiling at her, "I think it would be a help for us to have a story about Bee Confident. Do you have a story on that Bee? Maybe you could tell it to us this evening?"

Every eye was on Grandma! "Oh, Grandma, will you tell us about this Bee . . . maybe tonight . . . will you please," Don pleaded with real expectancy.

"Yes," Grandma hurriedly promised. "And maybe today as we are cleaning up the yard we can learn some more about Bee Confident."

Soon they had finished eating breakfast and Don went to help Grandpa with the chores. Joyce helped Grandma with the dishes and then they went out to help pick up the many twigs and branches that were all over the yard.

"I've never seen any storm make such a mess as this!" exclaimed Joyce as she helped Don carry a big branch to

Grandpa who was sawing or chopping them into lengths for the fireplace.

Later that afternoon a neighbor came with his chain saw to help Grandpa cut the big maple trunk into logs for the fireplace. When they had just a short stump left, Grandpa called to Don and Joyce. "How old do you think this tree was? I knew it had been planted when I was a small boy, but I had not really considered its age."

As Don and Joyce were hovering over the stump, Grandpa pointed. "See, you can tell how old this tree is by counting these little rings . . . beginning here at the center," Grandpa explained. "Let's count them together."

So they counted aloud until they had 58 rings. "Yes . . . that is about right. I must have been a boy about eight years old when my father planted this tree. It has given us wonderful shade all these years. Now it is gone. We will miss it very much," he said in an almost sorrowful tone.

It was a tired foursome who sat on the porch in the evening. It had been a most interesting, yet weary day of toil. "Now, Grandma, what about our story. Will you tell us what it means to Bee Confident?"

There seemed to be a smile of confidence upon Grandma's face as she settled back in the big old rocker and started the story-telling hour which the children had learned to love so dearly.

"All down through the centuries all who have really walked with God have developed a confidence, or learned to live with faith. But this came about through hardships that God permitted in order to develop confidence that He will provide and protect.

"The Bible tells us that David looked out one day at the host of wicked men that were encamped against him and he said: 'My heart shall not fear,' 'The Lord is my . . . salvation,' ' . . . in this will I be confident,' ' . . . He shall hide me in his sheepfold' " Psa. 27: 1, 3, 5.

"Now let me tell you a wonderful account of two missionaries who truly learned to be confident in the Lord.

"When missionary Von Asselt, A Rhenish missionary, first went to Sumatra in 1826 he found the natives near the coast savage and cruel.

"Twenty years before, two missionaries who had come to them with the gospel had been killed and eaten!

"Missionary Von Asselt and his wife were very lonely at first. They could not understand the language of the natives, but they did understand their hostile looks and gestures. They felt that they were surrounded by the power of darkness. Often in the night they had to get up and read the Word of God and pray to find relief from their fears.

"After two years they moved several hours journey inland to a tribe which was somewhat civilized and more

106

friendly. There they built a little house and life became
a bit more easy and cheerful.

"They had been in the new place a few months when
a man from the hostile district came to talk to them. After
he had chatted for a while with the missionaries, the man
asked, 'Teacher, I have a request. I want to have a look
at your watchmen close at hand!'

" 'What watchmen do you mean? I do not have any,'
said the missionary.

" 'I mean the watchmen whom you put around your
house at night to protect you.'

" 'But, I have no watchmen,' the missionary said again.
'I only have a boy and a cook who help me. They would
make poor watchmen.'

"The man from the hostile tribe looked at the missionary unbelievingly. He said, 'Do not try to make me
believe otherwise, for I know better. May I look through

your house to see if they are hidden there?'

" 'Certainly!' said the missionary. 'Look through it, but you will not find any watchmen.'

"So the man went in and searched every corner of the little house. Then he came out, very much disappointed.

" 'Now,' said the missionary, 'I want you to tell me about the watchmen you have seen around my house.'

"Then the native from the hostile tribe told this story. 'When you first came to us, we were very angry with you. We did not want you to live among us. We did not trust you. We decided to kill you and your wife. Night after night we went to your house to kill you, but when we came near the house there always stood close around it a double row of watchmen with shining weapons! We did not dare to attack them to get into your house. We were not willing to give up our plan to kill you, so we hired an assassin to do it for us!

" 'He laughed at us when we told him what we had seen and told us he had no fear of God or devil and would be only too glad to do the job for us!

" 'So one evening he marched ahead of us swinging his weapon over his head. When we neared your house, we let him go on alone while we remained behind. Very soon he came running back to tell us he dare not risk going through alone for there were two rows of big strong men standing close together and their weapons shone like fire!

" 'It was then we gave up our plan to kill you. Now tell me, where are these watchmen?'

"The missionary told the native that neither he or his wife had ever seen the watchmen. Then he got his Bible. Holding it open before the native, he said, 'This book is the Word of our great God. In this book He promises to guard and defend us. We believe this Book. We do not have to see the watchmen which God places around us. We know He is protecting us. But God has shown you the watchmen in order that you may learn to believe that He is the great and true God Who watches over and protects His children.' "

Grandma paused a moment. "Can you see how God helped these missionaries develop confidence in Him? It was not by taking them out of difficulty, but by protecting them in the midst of difficulty. So remember, Don and Joyce, when you hear this Bee buzzing, you are being taken through a difficult test so you can learn to Bee Confident."

"Oh! That was a wonderful story. Thank you Grandma . . . thank you." Joyce joined Don in the last thank you.

"And now, our little helpers, you are so tired. Run along to bed and we'll see you in the morning," Grandpa said, hiding a yawn!

The Best Story--Yet!

"LISTEN to the mocking bird!" exclaimed Joyce, early the next morning. "It sounds as if he would burst his throat. Sometimes his song is loud, and then again he whistles softly, like our canary."

As they listened, the bird whistled shrilly, like the cardinal; then he trilled like the canary, and chirped like the sparrow. He gave a call like the hen quail's, and sang a song exactly like the song of the bluebird. Then he twittered like a number of smaller birds, sang the song of the robin, and came back to the whistle of the cardinal.

"Did you ever hear such a wonderful song?" cried Joyce. "I could listen to him all day long."

"I like to hear him sing in the *daytime*, too," laughed Grandma; "but during the night I don't enjoy it so much.

Last spring the mocking birds built their nest in the same tree where that little fellow is singing now; and such music, all night long, during the time when they were nesting! It was beautiful, but it kept me awake many an hour when I should have been sleeping. Mocking birds usually build their nests near houses, to protect themselves from robbers."

"Robbers! What kind?" exclaimed Don.

"Sometimes larger birds; and sometimes cats, or snakes. You can always tell when a robber is about, by the fuss the old birds make. Last spring I heard a great commotion in that tree, and I went out to see what was the trouble. I looked about for a quite a while before I discovered the nest; and all the time, the birds were darting here and there and giving their sharp little cries of distress. When at last I found the nest, I saw a big black snake crawling toward it. I got the garden rake and pulled him loose from the limb; and when he fell to the ground, I killed the cruel thief."

Joyce stepped out into the yard, to get a better look at the little songster as he sat swinging at the top of the old apple tree. Just then he flew across the orchard and down to the creek, alighting among the willows along the bank.

That afternoon the children went to the creek, to see if there were any water lilies in bloom. As they neared the clump of willows, Don said, "Let's be quiet, and see if we can find the mocking bird." So they walked softly, and talked in whispers; but they did not catch a glimpse of the lovely songster. Suddenly Don stopped and pointed to a big green frog sitting on a lily pad in the middle of the creek.

"Oh-h-h!" exclaimed Joyce. Instantly there was a splash, and the frog was gone. There were splashes all around, as other frogs disappeared in the water.

The children hid behind the willows, and waited quietly for some time. Soon they saw a big green fellow swim toward the lily pad and climb up on it. Others began to swim about in the water, and a number of them came out along the bank.

Suddenly Joyce caught sight of something else, which made her forget the frogs. Just beyond the spot where the frog sat perched on a lily pad, there was a lovely water lily in bloom.

"O Don," she whispered, "do you think we can get it?"

"I'd rather have the frog than the lily," answered Don.

"Yes, but you can't get him, you know," said Joyce. "Will you help me to get to the lily?"

Don nodded, and came out from behind the willows where he had been crouching. Instantly there was another splash, and Mr. Froggie was gone. In a moment there was not a frog to be seen anywhere.

To get the lily, the children had to cross the creek and then step out on an old log. The creek was so shallow that they knew there was no danger of drowning, even if they should fall into the water; so Joyce steadied the log with her hands, while Don stood on it and reached for the lily. It took him some time to get it, for it had a tough stem which was very hard to break. But Joyce was so pleased when he handed her the beautiful lily, that he felt repaid for all his trouble.

About three o'clock the children found some empty spools and went to the corner of the orchard, and sat down in the cool shade of the lilac bush. Soon they were blowing many-colored bubbles and flying them in the air.

Tabby, Grandma's pretty Maltese cat, lay curled up in the shade. One of Don's bubbles lit on her back, where it swayed for a while, and then burst. By and by another lit on her nose, and burst immediately. The old cat jumped to her feet and began to sneeze. Then she sat down and washed her face with her paw, as if to say, "Thank you, I'd rather wash my face without any soap."

That evening, as they sat on the porch, Joyce said a little sadly, "It will not be long before we shall hear the noisy street cars again, instead of the katydids and the whippoorwills. Only one night more after this, and we shall be home."

"Yes," added Don—"only two more stories about the bees." He clambered up on to the arm of Grandma's rocking chair, while Joyce sat down at her feet.

"We're ready for our story, Grandma," said Don.

"All right," answered Grandma. "I shall tell you this time about a little bee called Bee Content. Its buzz is often heard among children at play, when things happen that no one can help. Some will not listen to it, and so they complain and make everyone about them miserable.

"Willie was a poor boy who lived on a farm. Although he had to work very hard, helping his father, he always went about whistling or singing. His clothes were old and patched; and he did not have things to play with, as other boys have. But he did not mind being poor, because he had parents who loved him dearly.

"One day when Willie was working in the field, he looked up and saw a great cloud of dust. A team was running away. The horses were hitched to a buggy; and as they came rushing toward him, the thought flashed into Willie's mind that he must try his best to stop them. A short distance down the road, there was a bridge. 'If the horses should run into the railing,' he thought, 'they would

tear the buggy to pieces, and perhaps hurt themselves.'

"The boy leaped over the fence, and braced himself; and as the horses came near, he grabbed one by the bridle and held on tightly. This was a very brave thing to do; for if he had missed catching hold, he must have been thrown under the horses' hoofs and trampled to death. His weight swinging on the horse's bridle soon stopped the team.

"Soon a man came running along the highway; and when he learned what Willie had done, he said, 'You are a brave boy. What do I owe you for your trouble?'

"Willie smiled his friendly smile as he answered, 'I did not stop the horses for pay, sir. I thought of the railing on the bridge; and I was afraid the horses would break the buggy, and hurt themselves.'

"Noticing that Willie's clothes were badly worn, the gentleman said, 'Will you not let me give you some money to buy clothes?'

" 'I have a better pair of shoes than these—and a better suit of clothes, for Sundays,' answered Willie. 'And these clothes are all right to work in.'

" 'But you will need some new books for school this fall,' said the gentleman.

" 'I have some books that were given to me,' replied the lad; 'and Mother glued in the loose leaves, so that I can use them very well, thank you.'

" 'Wouldn't you like to have a ball and bat?'

" 'I made a ball from some old old wool that Mother gave me,' answered Willie; 'and I whittled out a bat which answers the purpose very well.'

"The gentleman laid his hand on Willie's shoulder, saying kindly, 'My boy, I understand now why you have that smile; for you have learned a secret which few people know—the secret of contentment. I shall have to call you The Contented Boy.' And with that, he drove away.

"A few days later, a large box came to the village, addressed to Willie. The express agent sent word out to the farm, and Willie's father drove in to the village to get it.

"When Willie opened the box, he found a large card lying on top on which were written the words: *To the Contented Boy, From a Grateful Friend and Debtor.* He knew then that the box had come from the man whose team he had stopped a few days before.

"It contained a new suit of clothes, some shirts, overalls, stockings, a warm cap and mittens, and a new baseball and bat. When he lifted out the overcoat he felt in the pockets and discovered a five-dollar bill.

"How pleased Willie was! As he went back to his work

in the field, he whistled more cheerily than ever.

"But that was not all. At Christmas time, a wonderful bicycle came from his new friend. You will believe me when I tell you that he was the happiest boy in the country."

"That's the best story you have told us yet," said Don. "I think Willie was a brave boy."

"And he deserved everything he got," added Grandma; "for he had learned the secret of being content with a very little."

The Note That Fell

From The Window

BEFORE DON AND JOYCE came down for breakfast Grandma had received a phone call from Mrs. Brown.

She greeted the children with, "I've got a nice surprise for you today. Our neighbor, Mrs. Brown, who lives down the road, has her two grandchildren with her this summer. She called to ask if you would like to spend the day with them. There is Rex, who is about Don's age and Marita is about your age, Joyce. I told her I could call her after you had decided what you wanted to do."

"Oh yes," Joyce replied happily. She was always eager for new experiences. "I would like to play with Marita.

I'll take a couple of my new games along, and maybe I'll take the apron you are helping me make . . . and . . . why, Don, what's the matter with you?" Joyce asked with concern.

Don was very glum. He could never hide his feelings from anyone. It was evident he was not as eager as Joyce.

"Well," he began, "I was . . . I was planning to help Grandpa drive the cattle to the west pasture this morning. Besides I don't know Rex . . . and . . . well . . . maybe he won't like me or want to play the games I like . . . and maybe. . . . Do I really have to go?"

As they sat down at the breakfast table Grandpa looked at Don, but he said nothing. His piercing, but understanding look told Don a lot. He knew that Grandpa *did* understand how timid he was—especially in meeting new friends or visiting new places. And he also knew that Grandpa could look right back into his heart to see the real reasons. Don wished Grandpa would say something.

Finally Grandpa said, "Don, you are old enough to make your own choice. We will not insist that you go. I will wait until tomorrow to move the cattle if you want to help me." He paused a moment then continued, "but I do think it would be nice if Rex had someone to play with—especially since his sister will be with Joyce all day."

Don continued eating. He was thinking hard. Was it really fair to ask him to give up his sister to play with a girl they didn't even know. Was this really fair to *him*. Was it fair to ask *him* to play with someone he had never met?

As he looked up into the eyes of Grandpa those eyes seemed to say: "Don, I think you are a selfish boy who only thinks of himself, and only considers what will make him happy."

Deep inside Don knew that Grandpa was right. He also knew how often Joyce had to play the game he wanted. He had seldom given her the choice. As he finished his breakfast he continued to think. Everyone was quiet. They all seemed to be waiting for Don to make up his mind.

Then suddenly it seemed he knew exactly what he must do. It was as though an inner voice were saying to Don: "Those who belong to Me do not always think about themselves and what is best for them, but what will be best for others."

Don really wanted to go over to be with Rex, but he was still afraid of meeting new friends. Why didn't he ask the Lord to help . . . Don pondered. Wasn't that what he could expect of his New Shepherd . . . hadn't He promised to help him in the difficult things?

Don looked up and there was a new smile of confidence on his face as he announced: "I guess you can call Mrs. Brown and tell her we'll both be coming! I was afraid to go . . . well, I was not sure I wanted to meet Rex, but I've just asked the Lord to help me and I know He will."

That evening when they returned both Don and Joyce wanted to talk at once! Don was so excited and full of the day's happenings. Joyce could hardly get a word in to tell how much she had enjoyed playing with Marita.

When they finally settled down for their evening story, there was a twinkle in Grandpa's eye as he suggested, "Grandma, I've been waiting for you to tell your story about Cripple Tom. Don't you think tonight would be a good time to read that one?"

Grandma was already sitting with a small booklet in her hand. Looking up at Grandpa she replied, "I guess you have been reading my mind, because that is exactly the story I have chosen to read! Since we had our little episode at the breakfast table this morning which showed us how often we make choices that please us, and how often our lives are filled with *getting* instead of giving— well, I thought we should get acquainted with a little bee that needs to buzz in the ear of every boy and girl who belongs to the Lord. And not only children, but grown-up folk too, need to know this bee called BEE GIVING. Let me read this story to you:"

In one of the deplorable, miserable East London homes, in a dark, wretched room at the top of a house, lay a cripple boy, Tom. He had lain there for over two

years, greatly neglected and comparatively unknown. When quite young his parents had died, leaving him to the mercy of an aged relative whom he called "Granny."

Born a cripple, he had always been a sufferer. But as long as he was able, he had swept sidewalks on his crutches, or had done short errands to earn a few pennies. Soon after his parents' death Cripple Tom had to go to bed. Very grudgingly the old woman allowed him to occupy the top room of her house, which room he never left again!

His mother had taught him to read and write, but not knowing the truth herself, she had never told him of "Jesus and His love." Sometimes, however, on a snowy night, when the wind was blowing hard and cold, the lad had crept into the Mission Hall, not far distant, merely to get warm by the comfortable stove.

Numb with cold and weary in body, he really took little notice of what he heard on those nights. But now lying alone day after day, there came into his mind the memory of it, and by degrees he had a great longing to know more about God and to have a Bible of his own.

He knew that it was from the Bible that the speakers had gotten their knowledge—but that was all.

So summoning up all his courage he one day talked to Granny about it. But she only laughed and said, "Bibles aren't in my line: And what does a lad like you want with a Bible?" With this, the matter was dropped for a time, but Tom's desire to possess one did not grow less!

One day, however, up the creaking stairs came noisy, boisterous Jack Lee, the only friend the cripple had in the world.

"Hurrah! hurrah! I got a new box! I'm off North tomorrow! Came to say good bye, Tom," he cried with great excitement. Sitting down on the bed with Tom he added, "but I've got a real beauty present for yer, my lad!" Quickly he took from his pocket something wrapped in a greasy bit of brown paper. Tom raised himself on his elbows, not at all gladdened by the news he had heard. "A bright new shilling for you, Tom, lad. And you're not to spend it till yer wants suffin real pertikler!"

"Oh! Jack, you are good, but I want something *now* very very particular."

"Yer do? What?"

"I want a Bible!" Tom replied with great joy and excitement.

Jack just stood and looked at Tom a moment, then blurted out "A Bible! Well . . . I just never . . . whoever heard of a poor lad spending all that money on a Bible when I had to scrape months to save it!"

"Please don't be angry, dear Jack," cried Tom. "You're going away, and I shall be lonelier than ever. And oh, I do so want a Bible! Please get it, Jack—now— this very evening before the shop closes. Granny would never get it for me; she'd spend it on gin if I let it get into her hands."

"But what can yer want with a Bible, Tom, lad? Only scholars understand them there things," he answered rather crossly.

"Maybe so, Jack, but how very much I want it, for I must find out whether them there folks in that Mission Hall you and I sometimes used to go to, told the truth about Someone they called Jesus. Let it be your parting gift, Jack, and you will make me so glad!"

"Very well, lad, then I'll go; but I knows nothin'

about Bible-buyin'! Fisher has 'em at a shillin' for I saw 'em marked in the window when I used to go by."

"Go quick Jack, or the shop will be closed!" Tom begged anxiously.

Jack agreed very ungraciously, and descended the stairs less rapidly than he had mounted them. But he got over his disappointment before he returned with a beautiful 'shilling' Bible. "Fisher says I couldn't leave you a better friend, Tom, lad, and he declares the shilling couldn't be 'vested better. And he says It may be worth a thousan' pounds to yer. So it 'pears there's somethin' we ought to know about."

Tom's joy and gratitude was unbounded. "I know it, Jack. I know it!" Hugging the Book Tom exclaimed, "I'm happy now. Oh! how kind you were to save that shilling."

The lads never met again, but if Jack could only have known what a precious treasure that Holy Book became to his cripple friend, he would have been amply rewarded for the sacrifice he had made to save the shilling.

After a month's hard reading, Tom knew more about his Bible than many who have professed to study it for twenty years. He had learned the way of salvation; his only teacher being the Holy Spirit. He had learned also that obedience to God's will meant helping others to know the Lord Jesus.

"It won't do to keep all this blessed news to myself," he said. So he thought and thought until at last a simple, but very beautiful, work was decided on for his Lord. His bed was close by a low window. Somehow he got a pencil and paper. After asking the Lord to direct him, he wrote out different scripture texts, which he would fold, pray over, and then drop into the noisy street below. The notes were directed—

"To the Passer-by—Please Read."

Tom hoped that by this means someone might hear of the Lord Jesus and His salvation. This service of love, faithfully rendered, went on for some weeks, when one evening he heard a strange footstep on the stairs. Shortly a tall, well-dressed gentleman entered the room and took his seat by the lad's bedside.

"You must be the lad who drops texts from the window?" he asked kindly.

"Yes," said Tom brightening up. "Have you heard if someone got hold of one?"

"Plenty, lad, plenty! Would you believe it if I told you that I picked up one last evening, and God blessed it to my soul?"

"I can believe in God's Word doing anything, sir,"

said the lad humbly.

"And I am come," the gentleman continued, "to thank you personally."

"Not me, sir! I only does the writin'; He does the blessin'."

"And you are happy in this work for Christ?" the gentleman asked looking around the bare attic room.

"Couldn't be happier, sir," Tom answered smiling. "You see, I don't think nothin' of the pain in my back, for shan't I be glad when I sees Him, to tell Him that as soon as I know'd about Him I did all I could to serve Him?" Then looking up at the kind gentleman he asked, "I suppose you get lots o' chances to do something for the Lord."

With tears in his eyes he answered, "Ah! lad, but I have neglected them; but God helping me, I mean to begin afresh. At home in the country I have a sick lad dying. I had to come to town on pressing business. When I kissed him good-by he said, 'Father, I wish I had done some work for Jesus. I cannot bear to meet Him empty handed!'"

"These words stuck in my mind all day long, and the next day too, until the evening when I was passing down this street your little paper fell on my hat. I opened it, and read: 'I must work the works of Him that sent Me while it is day; the night cometh, when no man can work' John 9:4. It seemed like a command from heaven! It startled me, and brought me to my knees that night, and I could not sleep until I could sing—

'Oh! the cleansing blood has reached me,
Glory, glory to the Lamb!'

"I have professed to be a Christian for twenty-one years, my lad. When I made inquiries and found out who dropped these texts in the street and why it was done—

it so shamed and humbled me that I determined to go home and work for the same Lord and Master that you are serving so faithfully!"

Tears of joy were rolling down the lad's face. "It's too much, sir," he said; "altogether too much."

"Tell me, how did you manage to get the paper to start this, my lad?" the visitor asked.

"That warn't hard, sir. I jest had to talk with Granny and offered to give up my portion of milk she gives me most days, if she would buy me paper instead. You know, sir, I can't last long. The doctor says a few months of cold weather may finish me off, and a drop o' milk ain't much to give up for my blessed Jesus." Tom paused, then asked, "Are people happy who have lots to give Him, sir?"

The visitor sighed a deep sigh. "Ah! lad, you are a great deal happier in this wretched room making sacrifices for Jesus than thousands who profess to belong to Him, and who have time, talent and money, and do little or nothing for Him."

"That's because they just don't know Him, sir. Knowin' is lovin' and lovin' is doin'. It ain't love without!"

"You are right, Tom, my lad. But how about yourself. I must begin by making your life brighter. How would you like to end your days in one of those homes for cripple lads where you would be nursed and cared for, and where you would see the trees and flowers and hear the birds sing? I could get you into one not far from my home, if you liked, Tom."

The weary lad looked wistfully into the man's kindly face, and after a few moments of silenced answered: "Thank you sir; I've heard tell of 'em afore, but I ain't anxious to die easy when He died hard. I might get taken up with them things a bit too much, and I'd rather be a-lookin' at Him, and a-carryin' on this 'ere work till He comes to fetch me! Plenty of joy for a boy like me to have a mansion with Him up there through eternity."

The kind gentleman felt more reproved than ever. "Very well, my lad. Then I will see that you have proper food and all the paper you need while you live. Now, laddie, before I go I want you to pray aloud for me."

As he made the request the strong man knelt down by the dying boy's bedside, scarcely suppressing a sob as he covered his face with his hands.

There was an angelic light on the poor, pale, upturned face, as he said in a tone of the deepest reverence: "Lord Jesus, I know You're a-listen' and I'm much obliged to You for sending this friend here to cheer me in my work. Now, Lord Jesus, he's a bit troubled about not havin' worked for you enough in past days. Will You help him to see to it that there's nothin' left undone in the comin' days? And please, Lord, make him go straight away and tell them other rich men that they don't really love You if they aren't a-workin' for You.

"And I'm grateful to You, Jesus, for all the paper and the food that's a-comin' to me while I live. Maybe I'll hold out a bit longer to write these texts for You. Now, Lord Jesus, please bless this kind friend. I ask this for Your Name's sake."

There was a long pause and then the kind visitor said, "Amen!" He arose to shake hands with cripple Tom as he told him good-bye.

Before leaving London he made every arrangement for the lad to be cared for, and then with a gladder heart he went back to his beautiful country home and lived for Christ.

As soon as he could, he built a Mission Hall on his own grounds and preached Jesus to the villagers. When he confessed his sin of negligence towards them, and told them of his spiritual restoration, through the cripple boy and his text, many of them were led to the Lord Jesus.

News of the dying lad reached them from time to time. But it was not till winter had set in and the snow had fallen and covered the earth with its crystal whiteness, that they heard that the dear lad had gone to be with the Lord.

A few days later the gentleman received a parcel which contained Tom's much-prized and much-used Bible. What a precious treasure was that marked Bible! For when the cripple boy's friend loaned it to his youngest son to read, the careful marking, the short, simple prayers written by the cripple lad on the margin, and his dying wish on the fly-leaf, written about a week before his death, that "This Holy Book may be as great a friend to someone else as it has been to me," made such an impression on him that he gave himself to the Lord Jesus. And later on he went to Central Africa to witness for the Lord.

Grandma looked up as she finished reading. No one said a word. Finally Grandpa broke the silence. "I never hear that story but what I want to tell the Lord again I have been giving so very little to Him."

"I guess I never realized that a small boy or girl could do much for the Lord," Joyce added—wiping a tear from her eye.

"And me . . ." Don blurted, "I've been too busy just thinking about myself—like I was this morning. But I know the Lord is helping me to give more."

Grandma suggested that they should each pray, and then they slipped off to bed.

Everyone Ran
Away From Her

ALL MORNING the children helped Grandpa in the hayfield. We say helped, though actually they only rode on the wagon or the tractor as Grandpa and his neighbor hauled the fresh hay to the barn loft.

Don and Joyce had tried to place the bales of hay as the elevator lifted each one to the wagon, but they soon discovered they were too heavy for them. So they watched the stack grow taller and taller.

Don felt pretty grown-up when Grandpa showed him how to release the clutch and steer the tractor. "See Joyce," he called out, "I'm driving the tractor all by myself!"

"Another year, and you'll be able to drive the tractor for me," Grandpa encouraged him. This was great news for Don who was almost convinced that he would become a farmer when he grew up.

As they came in with another load of hay, they heard Grandma ringing the big old bell telling them it was time to eat. "Oh boy, food!" shouted Don as he and Joyce jumped from the wagon and raced to the house.

Grandma was waiting for them at the back door. After one quick look at them she exclaimed, "Well, it looks like you have had a great time this morning. I see you are really dirty from all the dust the wind has been blowing. Be sure to wash your hands and arms real well, then hurry in because I have something extra special for dinner you'll like.

Don was so anxious to eat that he had to be encouraged by Joyce to come back and do a complete job of washing up for dinner.

After a full afternoon of fun and excitement, the children were back to eat supper. "Don," Grandma tried to hide a smile as she looked over at him, "I believe you'll have to go back and wash some more. I'm afraid we'll lose our appetite looking at those dirty wrists and arms!" Grandpa nodded in agreement.

"Aw——!" And before he knew it, he had said something he had never said before. Somehow it seemed to just slip out. Indeed, Don was very tired, and now he was provoked. . . .

"Why Don!" Joyce exclaimed with a sisterly alarm. "I'm surprised at you! What would Mother and Daddy think. And besides now that we belong to God, you should never, never use His name in that way."

Don hung his head in shame. No one else needed to say a word. Big tears came to his eyes as he hurried off to finish the job of washing his hands and arms.

It was a sober faced boy that returned. As he looked up at the three, it was with a sob of sorrow he said, "Grandma, Grandpa . . . Joyce, I'm sorry . . . please forgive me. I really . . . well . . . it just slipped out before I realized what I was saying. I've already asked the Lord to forgive me. I guess I heard the neighbor using God's name today . . . and . . . "

"Yes, Don," Grandpa said gravely. "And I'm sorry that you have been exposed to that language throughout the day. Our neighbor is such a kindly helper, and he tries to control his swearing when he comes over, but there are times he gets upset and angry . . . and I guess he just forgets himself."

As they bowed their heads to give thanks for the food, Grandma added, "let us also ask that our memory will be cleared of all that is not good and clean."

How cool and refreshing the breeze was as Don and Joyce waited for Grandma to come out to the porch. They wondered what story she could tell them tonight.

They didn't have to wait long, for here she came with a book in her hand. "You know," she began, "I've been thinking how important it is for all of us who belong to the Lord to keep in the right company if we want to be clean. When we really love the Lord, we have an inner urge to keep our bodies clean, but we also want to keep our inner heart and mind clean.

"Some weeks ago I read a very interesting story about some children in Africa. I think I'll read it to you now—we'll call this lesson BEE CLEAN."

Lady Full of Joy, the missionary, was grieved because she had only ten fingers! In the brown and gold village there were ten times ten children who, as she walked through the village streets, wanted to hold one of them — all at the same time. The rest, who were left out, trailed behind her skirts like the wagging tail of a little dog.

"What could she do about not having more than ten fingers," the Lady Full of Joy wondered.

Suddenly she had a bright idea! Only brownies that had clean hands could hold hers, she decided. Most of

theirs had not been scrubbed in many a day, and her own were always black from their sticky little hands. They had learned in Sunday School to say:

"Who shall ascend into the hill of the Lord or
Who shall stand in His holy place?
He that hath clean hands and a pure heart."

Now, she decided they must put this verse into practice. So the very next day when they crowded about her she said, "Who has clean hands today? Only those who have scrubbed their fingers may hold mine!"

Every grimy little hand was held up and every little woolly head was bowed in shame. Then suddenly there was a dash for the brown mud huts with the golden grass roofs. In the dark corner of each of these was a gourd of water, which had been carried on the heads of the Mamus from the bubbling spring.

These few cups of water were all the family had during the day for cooking and scrubbing and bathing and drinking! No wonder the brownies were not very clean! Into the gourds went every little black hand. There was no soap and no towel, so out they dashed into the sunshine of the village street with hands dripping and faces triumphant.

Once again there was another scramble for the Joy Lady's fingers, and drops of muddy water splashed from the tips of little hands all over her starched white dress.

"This is worse than ever," thought the Lady Full of Joy. Then she had another idea.

"Children, you must go to the spring to bathe," she said firmly. "Only Jesus can give you a pure heart, but you yourselves must have clean hands before we say our verse next Sunday."

A week later, in the midst of the Bible story a small hand with tan palms scrubbed pink, was raised high.

"See, *Mamu*, I have clean hands," the brownie cried.

At once a dozen little hands were frantically waved and a chorus of children's voices called, "See, *Mamu*, we all have clean hands!"

It seemed the lesson of the previous week on "Clean Hands in a Holy Place" had taken effect.

Mujinga, however, sat silent. Mujinga was the little girl that the Lady Full of Joy especially loved because she was always on time to Sunday School and she always knew her verses.

Mujinga had gone to the bubbling spring early in the morning to bathe with the other little girls, but they had pointed at her and called her "*Muenu Nsudi*" and had run away from her. Hot tears blinded her eyes, and half way up the steep hill from the bubbling water she had stumbled and fallen in the deep white sand. The sticky grains clung to her and she looked like a walking sand pile!

In the path before her was a pretty white circle of heavy cardboard with nice black letters written on it. She could not read them, but she forgot the ugly name that her playmates had called her in the joy of finding a pretty treasure that looked almost like the yellow disk the white lady sometimes wore about her neck. Mujinga stripped a string of fronds from a little palm tree by the path and tied the white disk of cardboard with the black letters written upon it proudly about her neck. She walked up to the front seat so that all the children could see her new treasure.

The Lady Full of Joy looked at Mujinga in surprise because she did not raise her hand. What she saw would have made her laugh if Mujinga had not looked so sad. There she sat on the front seat, her little body covered with sand and her little hands grimy from her fall, but round her neck was a cardboard milk-bottle stopper upon which was written in big letters, WASH AND RETURN!

After the children's meeting was over and all of the little ones with their hands scrubbed clean had gone, Mujinga slipped up to the desk where the white Mamu was packing the bright pictures and putting away the song books.

"Mamu," she said wistfully, "look at my hands. I've tried to scrub them clean, but there are some spots I can't wash off. The other children saw them this morning and called me *Muenu Nsudi* and ran away from me. Mamu, am I a *Muenu Nsudi*? Why won't these spots wash off?"

All of the joy suddenly went out of the Joy Lady's heart, for the strange white spots on little Mujinga's hands were those of a leper! The children were right, for *Muenu Nsudi* means, A LEPER!

"Mujinga," she said gently, "you must go home with me at once to see the white doctor. If those spots are what I think they are, the children were right . . . you are a leper. But you must not cry for there is a lovely home for you," she continued as she put her arm around her slight shoulders.

"Do you know that the doctor can give you some medicine made from that big round fruit that looks like a grapefruit covered with brown velvet? Inside it looks like soft white soap filled with nuts, and inside these nuts is a golden oil that will help to make you well. And do you know that he can wash those spots off with an acid that will make them go away?" Lady Full Of Joy spoke softly as she looked into the frightened eyes of the little brownie.

"But Mujinga," she smiled, "do you know what you have hung around your neck?"

"No *Mamu*, I found it in the path this morning and I thought it was pretty because it looked like what you wear about your neck sometimes."

"Mujinga, that is a milk bottle stopper from the foreign country, and on it is written in our language, "Wash and Return"! I'm glad you found it and wore it, Mujinga, for now since many who love the Lord Jesus have built our Christian Leper Camp, you can have proper food, care and medicine and you can be made well there. While there they, too, will teach you how to have a pure heart. I'm sure they will *wash and return* you, so don't cry any more little one. Let us bow our head and thank the Lord Jesus for such a nice place provided by those who love Him and you."

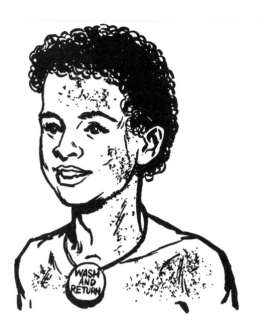

Grandma closed her book. Everyone sat quietly for a moment.

Don broke the silence, "I guess I'll never again complain about having to wash. Boy, wouldn't it be awful to have spots you couldn't wash away . . . "

"And to be taken away from home and friends because you might . . . might infect others," Joyce added.

"But what is even worse," Grandma spoke thoughtfully, "is that people who do not know the Lord as their Saviour and Shepherd have never been cleansed from their sin, and in God's sight that is worse than leprosy."

"Really? Oh, how glad I am that I belong to Him," Don was quick to reply.

"And I'm glad He has made me clean inside," Joyce joyfully announced. "And we'll both do our best to keep clean on the outside, won't we Don," she said with a big knowing smile."

When Things
Go Wrong

BECAUSE IT WAS many miles to the nearest city, Grandpa and Grandma did not go very often. But today was the day they had planned for shopping.

Don and Joyce were very excited. The very thought of spending the whole day in the various stores was most inviting and you can be sure they had everything ready for an early start.

"You have been such good helpers these days, I want to give each of you a five dollar bill," Grandpa said handing each a crisp new bill as they were getting into the car. "Perhaps you might buy some clothes for school or . . ."

"Oh thank you Grandpa," Don interrupted. "I know exactly what I want . . . I'll buy a new light and horn for my bike!"

"And I want to buy a sweater. You know, one just like Marita was wearing when I visited her," added Joyce with great anticipation.

"Well, you may each choose whatever you wish," Grandma smiled as she closed the car door. "We have been so happy to have you with us and also thankful for your help."

Soon they were walking down the main street going from store to store. Joyce had already found her sweater— a pink one just like she had wanted. But Grandpa and Don were still looking for the light and horn for the bike.

"Across the street is another store," Grandma pointed. "Maybe you can find what you want over there."

When they reached the window, Don saw the light and horn he was wanting—and it was only four dollars, which meant that he still had one dollar left!

With Don's light purchased, they walked down the street. Though Grandpa encouraged him to wait, at least until they got to the car, he just had to have one look at his light! So right on the street he opened the box then quickly put the light back. How he would enjoy putting it on his bike when he got home—he could hardly wait!

"Now that the children have their money spent," Grandpa kidded, "why don't you take Joyce to the market for the groceries, Grandma, while Don and I go to the hardware for some shopping. Don, perhaps you can leave that light with Joyce and Grandma. We'll have enough to carry from the hardware store—and they'll have all their things in a shopping cart when we meet them."

So Grandpa and Don started off together. Don was still planning what he would buy with his remaining dollar

—maybe a ball, or a new notebook for school . . . or
. . . "Say," he puzzled, "where is that dollar? Must be
in my other pocket." He quickly pushed his hand into
the pocket, but it wasn't there!

"Grandpa," he cried, "I think I've lost my dollar!
I . . . well I thought it was right here in this pocket,"
he pointed. They stopped walking while Don searched
again through all his pockets.

"When the clerk gave me my change, I had exactly
one dollar bill left and I put it right here in this pocket
. . . I just know I did, but it's gone . . . Grandpa, it's
gone! Can't we go back and look for it? Maybe I might
have dropped it in that store and maybe they have found
it and are keeping it for me," he added hopefully.

So they carefully retraced their steps back to the store
—stopping every place they had been since buying Don's
light. But no one had found the dollar! To make matters
worse, when they got to the market where Joyce and
Grandma were waiting, Don had still another disappointment. Somehow, they didn't know just how, while
Joyce was carrying Don's light, it had fallen out of the
box to the pavement. Joyce tried to explain it all, but
Don quickly grabbed the box to look for himself. There
it was— the glass was broken, but even worse, the plastic
housing was also broken!

"Oh Joyce, how could you," Don wailed. "Why
weren't you more careful. Didn't you realize the end of
the box was open!"

Poor Don, as he turned dejectedly, tears were falling
down his cheeks. What a day! The day in the city he
had so looked forward to had become a big disappointment. First he had lost his dollar and now Joyce
had dropped his light. No one could cheer him. No one
could understand his problems! How could such things

140

happen to him—all in one day!

He sat glum and silent all the way home. Of course he could not blame anyone for losing his dollar. But he could hardly forgive himself for being so careless; he could hardly forgive Grandpa for insisting that he leave the light with Joyce and Grandma, or could he forgive Joyce for being so careless.

And even Grandma . . . yes, she could have watched over his sister Joyce so she would not have made that silly mistake! Of course he didn't say all this to them, but his attitude and his manner really did express what he was thinking. He was just plain put-out with everybody!

Don helped unload all the day's purchases when they got back. Joyce tried, in every way that a sister could, to show her sorrow and sympathy for poor Don, but he was not to be comforted! He just sulked and complained.

All afternoon Grandma had been giving much thought to the story she might have for the children in the evening. As the children came in and sat down she couldn't help but notice Don's face.

"Don," she said thoughtfully as she looked into his sad face, "this has been a very disappointing afternoon for you. But neither has it been a happy one for the rest of us. When you are disappointed, we are too! Tonight I want to read a story about a girl named Becky who was also very unhappy, but who learned a very important lesson through her experience. Grandma began reading:

Becky looked out of her window. She really felt sorry for herself. She wrestled with the sling that held her broken arm, then twisted her bandaged leg to find another position. Just then her mother came into the room carrying a glass of cold milk and some warm cookies. But Becky only turned her head and appeared to not notice her mother.

How could she ever forgive herself for listening to that dare from the children? She would never forget that day—a day when she had been riding her bike with her brother and the other boys and girls in the block. Someone had decided they should try going down the steep hill over on Wilson Avenue. So they had all raced over to try it.

Indeed it was a dangerous and bumpy hill, but it sounded like so much fun! She remembered the look on her brother's face as she started down. It was as though he were saying: Becky, you know Dad said we were never to ride our bikes down this hill. But she had ignored him, and accepting the dare had started down the steep hill!

The rest of the story you can imagine. She did not need to tell her father and mother she had raced some of the boys and girls down the steep hill on Wilson Avenue. Becky lost control of her bike as she picked up more and more speed, and the bumps of the road swung her over to the ditch where she fell in a heap.

It seemed every bone must have been broken—and then she passed out to awaken in the hospital some time later.

The weeks in the hospital passed by rapidly and now she was home. The broken bone in her arm had mended rapidly and the long bone between her knee and her ankle was also mending. The doctor had said that although it was a serious break, yet she would soon be able to walk and run with the other children in her block.

But Becky was not at all her cheerful self. Everyone who knew her realized that she was unusually quiet. In fact, she only answered questions and seemed quite

142

unwilling to talk with anyone who came to visit!

Her parents were concerned, but imagined it must be quite difficult for an active girl of twelve to be confined to her bed and chair all day when she really wanted to be in school with her friends. They felt Becky would change when she got home, but instead she had become even more sulky and disagreeable. Indeed this was so unlike Becky; they kept hoping that every day would bring a change.

Now three weeks had passed and Becky still refused to even try to walk!

"Doctor says you must begin to take some steps, dear," her mother pleaded as she tried to encourage her to get up from the chair.

But Becky made no move or effort. She just sat staring out of the window.

Her mother remembered that the doctor had told her

that Becky would never walk again if she didn't try. He had said they must do whatever was necessary to get her to move out of her chair, because the longer she waited the harder it would be for her to use her leg muscles.

She would try once again. "Becky, dear, won't you just stand and lean on me—I'll help you take just a step or two."

But Becky stubbornly refused to even accept her mother's offer.

That evening her father came in to sit by her side. Surely if anyone could encourage Becky to take a step, he could. He told her how glad they were she had not been hurt any worse, or that none of the other children were seriously hurt in that foolish escapade.

Becky sat silent for a few minutes then turning to her father she said, "But Dad, there's no use in trying, I know I'll never walk again!"

"But Becky, dear," he spoke softly, "you don't realize how many people have been hurt much worse than you, and they have returned to a normal life. Surely you can expect the same. And besides, we all have asked the Lord to help you and He will if you'll just try."

"Well, God certainly didn't give me much help the day I got hurt," Becky said bitterly as she turned her face to the wall.

"Why dear, surely you can't mean that God is to blame for your being hurt?" he asked as he put his arm around her trembling shoulders.

"But God let me get hurt, didn't He?" she argued. "Haven't I heard you say that if we have faith in God, He will take care of us? It doesn't look like He took very good care of me that day, did He?" Becky questioned.

"Becky," her father spoke gently, "I think you should

see that God took very, very good care of you that day. If He had not taken care of you, you surely would have been hurt much worse—maybe even killed.

"You see, my dear, you were doing something you knew was wrong, something you had been told many times not to do because it was so dangerous. We cannot do things that are dangerous and wrong and think God will keep us from getting hurt. In your case, it is not

a matter of having faith, but it is a matter of obeying what you know is right."

He paused as he waited for her to speak. Becky sat quietly—she was thinking. Tears came to her eyes, but smiling she said, "Yes, I suppose you're right. I knew I should not have gone down that hill on my bike. I knew I should not have listened to the others who dared me. You're right, Dad, I guess God did take care of me, very good care, or I suppose I would have been hurt much worse—or even killed."

Just as Becky finished talking Mother walked in. "Oh Mother," she smiled as she reached out for her hand, "I've been so mean and disagreeable these past weeks—and mostly because I was put-out with God. I see how wrong *I've* been in my attitude. I felt He hadn't treated me right, but now I see it was *I* who had not treated Him right! I see it was not for me to forgive Him for not taking care of me, but that I should ask His forgiveness for not doing what was right."

Looking at both of her dear parents with tears in her eyes, she asked, "Will you both forgive me for dis-obeying you?"

"Of course we will," they both answered with joy.

"And if you will just trust Him, the Lord will give you strength and desire to walk again. Once our heart attitude is right, we can expect God to put strength in our legs," father added.

Suddenly the phone rang and father was called to answer it. Becky sat quietly for a moment and then motioned, "I'm ready now, Mother, if you'll just come over and help me a little!"

In a few minutes Becky had taken her first steps. She was weak and wobbly, but she had the will to try and that was a good beginning.

146

Now that Father had helped Becky to see that God had really blessed, not forsaken, her at the time of the accident, there was once again a song in her heart and a smile on her face.

Later that evening with the help of her father, she took ten more steps. Her brother stood by and cheered her on. "Oh, Sis, that's really wonderful!" he exclaimed as he cried and danced about for joy.

"Yes, brother," she smiled as she sat down, "I think I must even ask God to forgive me for blaming you! All these days I've been sitting feeling sorry for myself . . . and I'd even gotten around to blaming you for not stopping me from starting down that terrible steep hill! Now I see there are many lessons we learn in life, but the hardest one is to really be honest with ourselves and not to blame everyone else for what goes wrong."

Grandma looked into Don's eyes as she closed her book. All through the story she knew he had been thinking. It seemed the truth had made its way into his heart.

He smiled back at her. "I guess you've really described me in that story, Grandma. I have been feeling so sorry for myself and have been blaming everyone else for my troubles . . . but really, I'm the one who has been at fault."

"And Don," Joyce looked up to say, "I really am sorry that I dropped your headlight . . . I'm the one who spoiled part of your day . . ."

"Oh, Joyce, I forgive you . . . I know you didn't mean to drop it. And I'm sorry I've been so grumpy and disagreeable all day long, Grandma and Grandpa. Will you please forgive me?"

"You're forgiven, my boy," Grandpa said covering a big yawn with his hand. "I believe this has finally been a good day for all of us."

The Man Who
Could Not Shoot

ANOTHER MORNING came; the morning of the last day Joyce and Don were to spend on the farm. They followed Grandma about the house, eager to do something to help. After the usual work was done, and they had taken turns at the churning, Grandma said she would make cookies to pack in their lunch-basket the next day.

So she gathered together eggs, sugar, flour, milk, butter, baking powder, and spices. Quickly she made the dough and rolled it out on the board. The children stood close to her, watching as she cut out the dough in different shapes.

She made quite an army of cookie men; and after they were baked, she covered them with icing. She made their eyes out of cinnamon drops; also the buttons down their vests.

"Aren't they lovely?" cried Joyce. "Put plenty of them in our lunch-basket tomorrow, won't you, Grandma? Then we can take some home to Mother and Daddy."

148

"Yes," said Grandma, "and there will be enough for your little friends, too."

In the afternoon the children's trunk was brought out, and Grandma helped them to pack. There were so many things they wanted to take home with them, that this was quite a task. At the last moment, just as Grandma was ready to close the trunk, Don ran and got the kite that Grandpa had made. "Maybe Daddy will know how to make it fly," he said. But there was no room for it in the trunk, so he had to take it back to the woodshed.

"I can put it away in a safe place," he said. "It will be waiting for us when we come back next summer."

That evening the children did all they could to help Grandpa with the chores. They gathered the eggs, pumped water, filled the wood-box, and did many other things.

"You are certainly fine little helpers," said Grandpa when they had finished.

"When you get home," added Grandma with a smile, "you must tell Mother and Daddy that we need you to help us on the farm."

"We will," promised the children with beaming faces.

When they had gathered on the porch for their last evening together, Joyce stole up to Grandma's chair and said softly, "Tonight you must tell us the very best bee story that you know."

"It couldn't be better than the one about Bee Content," said Don.

"I shall tell you about the bee that is perhaps the most important of all," said Grandma thoughtfully. "It does wonderful things for those who listen to its buzz; but those who refuse to listen are sure to be sorry afterward. It is called Bee Prayerful."

The children were eager to hear the story, so Grandma began at once:

"William Sutherland was a boy who lived in the state of Maryland. When he was thirteen years old, he gave his heart to God and became a Christian. After that, he would often steal away alone and spend a few minutes talking to God.

"When he was fourteen, William began to work in the bank as an errand boy. The banker soon found that he was honest, and trusted him with large sums of money. One of his errands was to carry the pay roll to a mill town several miles away. He made this trip every two weeks; and he always set out in the afternoon, and returned the following morning.

"There were no automobiles in those days, and no good roads. William had to ride a pony, leaving the main highway and riding over a trail that had been blazed through the forest.

"As he started out one afternoon, his mother said to him, 'Son, I'm afraid to have you carry so much money over that lonely trail.'

" 'Oh, there is no reason to worry, Mother,' replied the lad cheerfully, as he swung into the saddle. 'You know I have always made the trip safely before.'

" 'Yes,' replied the good woman, 'but I feel fearful today. I shall be praying for you while you are on your way.'

"William waved to her, as he turned his pony about and started on his journey. He had placed the pay roll in his saddle bags; and as he looked at them he said to himself, 'How glad I am that my master trusts me with so much money.'

"He whistled and sang, as he rode along; but as he neared the lonely forest trail, a strange feeling of fear came over him. He reined in his pony and sat still for some time, wondering just what he ought to do. Then Bee Prayerful began to buzz about his ears. He had heard its little voice many times before, and he had learned always to listen and obey. He rode on to the spot where he must leave the highway and set out upon the forest trail; and then he slipped from the saddle and knelt down beside the bushes growing there.

" 'Dear God,' he said aloud, 'I don't know why, but I feel very much afraid. Take care of me, as I ride through this lonely place. I believe You will, because You have written in Your Book, "I will never leave thee, nor forsake thee." '

"And as William knelt there, alone with God, all feeling of fear melted away. He arose, mounted his pony, and rode on with a light heart.

"The mill men knew he was coming, for they could hear his cheerful whistle before his pony came into view. He gave the pay roll to the foreman, spent the night in the little town, and the next forenoon returned safely to his home.

"His mother met him at the door. 'Son,' she said, 'something peculiar happened to me yesterday while you were away. I was very busy, but a little voice seemed to tell me that I ought to stop my work and pray for you. I felt that you were in danger, and that I should ask God to keep you safe. So I laid my work aside, went into my room and knelt down, and stayed there until I was sure that you were quite safe.'

"Then William told her how he had felt just before he reached the lonely forest trail, and how he had knelt down among the bushes and asked God to protect him. After that, they often talked about this strange happening, and wondered what it could mean.

"William worked in the bank for quite a while, and then he went away to college. After he had graduated, he became a minister. Soon after this, God called away his good mother to her home in Heaven.

"One day William received a letter stamped with the postmark of a town in a distant state. 'I am very ill,' said the writer, 'and the doctor says I shall never recover. I must see you, as I have something very important to tell you before I am called away to meet my God. Please come to me as quickly as possible.' There was no name written at the end of the letter. It was signed, 'A friend.'

"William turned the letter over and over in his hand. He knew no one in that far-away place, and for a time he was very much puzzled. Then he did as he had been in the habit of doing for many years—he slipped away to spend a few moments alone with God. And a voice in his heart kept saying, 'Go; someone is in need, and your work is to minister to every soul who asks for help.'

" 'But whom shall I ask for, when I arrive?' asked William, still preplexed. And the voice answered, 'Only go; God will take care of the rest.'

"Hastily packing a few things in his traveling bag, William boarded a train and started for the town in the far-distant state. Arriving at the end of his journey, he stepped out upon the station platform. He was astonished when a gentleman came up to him and said courteously, 'Is this Reverend Sutherland?'

" 'Yes,' replied the minister, 'I am he.'

" 'I have been sent to meet you, sir,' said the stranger. 'I have met every train during the past week. Will you come with me?'

"A few minutes later he led the minister into a darkened room where a sick man lay. As they tiptoed into the room, he looked up eagerly, and his breath came fast. Holding out his hand, he asked in a feeble voice, 'Is this Reverend Sutherland?'

" 'It is,' said the minister gently, clasping the thin white hand. 'Where have I met you before, my friend—and what can I do for you now?'

" 'You have never met me before,' said the sick man, and his voice sank to a whisper. 'I saw you only once and that was many years ago. But I have kept track of your whereabouts all these years. I have sent for you now, sir, because—I am dying.'

"The sick man sank back upon his pillows and rested a moment; then, fixing his large eyes on the minister's face once more, he went on:

" 'Mr. Sutherland, one afternoon many years ago you were entrusted with a large sum of money to take to the foreman of a certain mill. In a wild and lonely spot, you slipped from your saddle and knelt down by some bushes and asked God to protect you. Do you remember it?'

" 'As if it had been yesterday,' said the minister. 'But, my good friend—what do you know about it?'

" 'Far more than you do,' said the sick man sadly. '*I heard that prayer.* I was crouching among the bushes

nearby, with my rifle pointed at your heart. I had planned to kill you, take the money, and ride away on your pony. But while you were praying something white seemed to pass between us; I did not know what it was, but I believed that God had sent it to protect you. I sat in those bushes, too weak to pull the trigger, and watched you ride away—perfectly helpless to do any harm to you. But it has haunted me ever since—the thought of what I wanted to do, and what I should have done if God had not answered your prayer. I could not meet God without telling you all this. Can you forgive me?'

"Again William grasped the hand of the dying man, saying in a husky voice, 'My friend, as God has forgiven my sins, I freely forgive you. Ask now for God's forgiveness, and be at peace.'

"The minister stayed with the man for some time, talking and praying with him; until at last the light shone in his dark soul, and God forgave his sins.

"He died soon after that, and William Sutherland was asked to preach his funeral sermon. He chose as his text those words from the book of Proverbs: 'Trust in the Lord with all thine heart; and lean not unto thine own understanding. In all thy ways acknowledge him, and he shall direct thy paths.' "

The children sat very still for some time, after Grandma had finished her story. "I think Bee Prayerful is the best of all," said Joyce at last. "I shall remember that story as long as I live."

"I hope you will, dear," said Grandma. "No matter where you go—no matter how busy you are—always listen to the gentle buzz of Bee Prayerful."

"We will, Grandma," said the children soberly.

"And now," said Grandma, "it is bedtime for two little folks who will have to be up bright and early in the morning. You know the train leaves at eight o'clock."

"Good-night, katydids and whippoorwills," murmured Don a little drowsily. "We shall come back to hear you sing again next summer."

With that, two tired children crept upstairs and tumbled into bed; and very soon they were in the Land of Dreams.

Home Again!

THE SUNLIGHT was streaming in at their bedroom windows, when Joyce and Don awoke the next morning. They dressed quickly, and ran down to watch Grandma pack their lunch for the trip home. At the breakfast table, they talked of all the nice times they had had during the past few weeks; and they promised to persuade Mother and Daddy to come with them to the farm next summer.

When everything was ready, Grandpa lifted the little trunk to his shoulder and carried it out to the car; and soon they were on their way. When they reached the station Grandpa bought the tickets, checked the little trunk, and gave the children a story book to read on the train. Dear Grandpa and Grandma! They always knew just what to do to make the children happy.

As the train whistled in the distance, Don caught Grandpa's hand and held it tight. Joyce threw her arms around Grandma and whispered,"Dear Grandma. I love you! And I've had such a happy time!"

The train pulled up, and the conductor called, "All aboard!" After Grandpa had helped them on to the train, and had gone back to the station platform, the children waved and threw kisses through the window. As the train moved away, they pressed their faces to the window and watched Grandpa and Grandma as long as they could. But they soon were left behind, the train moved faster, and the little village passed out of sight. Happy vacation days on the farm had come to an end.

For a few moments the children had to fight to keep back the tears. Then Joyce opened the book that Grandpa had given them, and soon their loneliness was forgotten.

There was a story about a little lame dog that came to a man's house one cold winter night and whined about the door. He let it in, bound up its foot, and gave it some food and a comfortable place to sleep.

The man liked the dog so well that he decided to keep it. One night, when everyone was asleep, the house caught fire; and the dog awakened the man in time to save the whole family from burning to death.

There were stories about cows and horses; and a long, long one about the interesting animals to be seen at the zoo.

One story was so funny that when Don read it, he burst out laughing; and the other passengers looked at him and smiled. It was about a mischievous monkey at the zoo. One day a gentleman who wore a wig came by, carry-

ing his hat in his hand. The monkey reached through the bars and caught hold of his wig, pulling it off his head.

When it was time for lunch, Joyce opened the basket that Grandma had packed for them. They spread out a napkin on the seat in front of them, and ate their lunch off this "table" in the most grown-up fashion. Grandma had tucked in several surprises; and how good the cookie-men tasted!

In the middle of the afternoon they began to pass through the suburbs of the city, and soon familiar sights came into view. When the train backed into the station, there stood Mother and Daddy waiting for them.

"O Mother," cried Joyce with a bear hug, "I've had a good time, but I'm so glad to see you again!" Don, big boy that he was, had jumped into Daddy's arms. Soon the trunk had been placed in the car, and they were driving toward home.

"What did you enjoy most of all, during your vacation?" asked Mother, as they were eating supper that evening.

"Fishing," replied Don quickly—"and catching the big turtle."

Joyce did not answer; she sat quite still, with a far-away look in her eyes.

"And what did my little girl like best of all?" asked Mother at last.

"O Mother," said Joyce, her eyes shining, "I was happy every minute—even when the old turkey gobbler was chasing me around the tree. But what I liked best was to sit out on the porch in the evenings, and listen to the katydids and whippoorwills, and watch the stars come out one by one. And then, it was so nice to sit close to Grandma's old rocking-chair and listen to her stories about the Hive of Busy Bees."

Now a Sequel:
Another Hive of Bees

I thought We had Warned You!	**Bee Careful**
A Lesson He Never Forgot	**Bee Orderly**
Fun...Catching Butterflies	**Bee Thoughtful**
Spelling Wasn't Important...Until...	**Bee Diligent**
Do Birds Play Games?	**Bee Devoted**
Making a Scrapbook	**Bee Neat**
"Our Grandpa is the Greatest!"	**Bee Thorough**
When the Robin Sings the Old Song	**Bee Unselfish**
Poor Marco Was Disappointed	**Bee Determined**
The Motto on the Wall	**Bee Resolute**
He Knew His Master's Voice	**Bee Loyal**
The Trick that Boomeranged!	**Bee Truthful**
Learning the Hard Way	**Bee Teachable**
A Difficult Decision	**Bee Consecrated**
Watching the Cocoon	**Bee Patient**
A Happy Visit	**Bee Confident**
Learning to Assume Responsibility	**Bee Useful**
It Took Courage to Tell	**Bee Honest**
"We're All So Rich"	**Bee Appreciative**
A Picnic at the Zoo	**Bee Content**
Where's the Butterfly?	**Bee Thankful**